BLACKMAILED
BY
TAFFY SINCLAIR

1 *

"Jana Morgan," I said to the face in the mirror. The bell would ring any second, and I was the only person left in the girls' bathroom, so I knew no one would hear me talking to myself or see the big, dopey grin I was wearing. "Your life is just about as perfect as it can get, and it's all because of Randy Kirwan. He likes you and NOT Taffy Sinclair!"

Randy is the kindest, most sensitive, and most wonderful boy in the whole wide world, and last Saturday he proved how much he likes me. He kissed me! It happened on the way home from pizza at Mama Mia's after his football game. I watched my dopey grin

1

get bigger than ever at the thought of that kiss, and I felt tingly all over.

Just then the bathroom door shot open and Beth Barry stuck her head inside. "Come on, Jana. You look gorgeous enough already. You'd better hurry up. It's time for the bell."

"I'll be there in a minute," I said in a dreamy voice. "I just want to brush my hair one more time before I see Randy."

Beth gave me a disgusted look and left. I already *knew* that it was time for the bell. That's why I was the only one left in the girls' bathroom. Everyone else had gone to class. I didn't care, even though I knew that Wiggins, my sixth-grade teacher, got angry whenever anyone straggled in late on Monday morning. I stood there anyway, smiling at myself in the mirror. Not only was everything going super with Randy, but Taffy Sinclair had failed one more time to take him away from me.

Taffy Sinclair is my enemy. We are rivals for everything at school, and in fifth grade we even had clubs against each other. She has long blond hair and big blue eyes and, as much as I hate to admit it, she's the most beautiful girl in Mark Twain Elementary. But she is also hateful and stuck-up. We are rivals for everything, and if that weren't bad enough, she flirts with all the boys, especially with Randy Kirwan. Actually, she had a big crush on Randy, and during the romance machine disaster she even tried to convince everybody that he liked her better than me.

The dopey grin disappeared as I thought about Taffy Sinclair, so I ran the brush through my hair and promised myself that I wouldn't let her spoil my good mood.

Suddenly the last bell rang. Panicking, I stuffed the brush into my jacket pocket and grabbed for my notebook on the shelf below the mirror. I wish I hadn't done that. I wish I had just reached for that notebook very slowly. And I wish I had taken hold of it firmly with both hands, because if I had, my life wouldn't have turned from perfect one instant to miserable the next.

I was in such a hurry that instead of picking up my notebook, I knocked it onto the floor. The last bell had stopped ringing by then and the place was so deathly quiet that it sounded like a blast from a cannon when it hit the concrete floor. Stuff flew out of it and shot off in every direction. Loose papers. Ballpoint pens. Paper clips. All kinds of things slid under the sinks, under the partitions around the stalls—everywhere.

At first, I just stood there looking at the mess. I couldn't believe that I had stuffed that much into one notebook. But then I remembered that I was late for class and that I would have to walk into the room in front of Randy and Taffy Sinclair and everybody. Wiggins would be on the warpath and demand to know why I was late. Only she would call it tardy.

I jumped into action, scrambling around and picking up things as fast as I could. I scooped up papers and pencils and paper clips and crammed them back into my notebook any way they would fit. I would put them where they belonged later. Right now I had to get to class.

My heart was pounding as I stood up and looked around one last time for anything I had missed. I started to leave when something red caught my eye. It was sticking out from behind a toilet in one of the stalls, and it could only be one thing. My favorite ballpoint pen. I sighed, half of me glad that I hadn't missed it and the other half wishing that I could hurry up and get out of there. I had wasted too much time already. I could almost hear Wiggins screaming at me when I walked into that sixth-grade room.

I pushed open the door to the stall and reached down to pick up my ballpoint pen. I stopped, my hand still in midair as I saw that my pen wasn't the only thing behind that toilet. There was something small and dark and oblong. It looked like a wallet. I forgot all about my ballpoint pen and picked up the other thing instead.

It WAS a wallet. A nice one, made out of leather. Not a vinyl one like most kids had. A creepy feeling came over me as I stared at it. What would somebody's good leather wallet be doing behind a toilet in the girls' bathroom? It couldn't have just accidentally fallen that far behind the toilet. It looked as if someone had hidden it there.

My creepy feeling was getting worse. I wanted to look inside and see if somebody's name was in it, but the last bell had already rung. Wiggins would go berserk if I came in any later.

I pushed the wallet down as far as I could into my jacket pocket, fitting it underneath my brush. I'd look at it at recess. Or maybe at noon. Then I'd decide what to do. I was almost out in the hall when I remembered my red ballpoint pen, and I dashed back into the stall and grabbed it. Then I hurried as fast as I could to my room.

I opened the door and tiptoed inside, trying to be as quiet and unnoticeable as possible. Wiggins looked up, but she didn't yell. I couldn't believe it. She just frowned at me over the top of her wire-rimmed glasses, told me to take my seat, and asked me if I realized that I was tardy, which of course I did. I should have known that there was only one reason she would treat being tardy so calmly. She had something else on her mind.

She didn't talk about it right away, though. She took roll, collected lunch money, made announcements, and did all the things she does on a normal day. In fact, things were so normal that I almost forgot about the wallet hidden in the bottom of my jacket pocket— that jacket I was still wearing because I hadn't had time to go to my locker before I came to class.

Something else took my mind off the wallet, too. Randy Kirwan. As soon as I sat down, he turned around and gave me his 1,000-watt smile, which always makes my heart do at least a hundred flip-flops. I smiled back, glad that I had taken time to brush my hair.

It was the first time I had seen him since Saturday, and I blushed when I thought about that kiss. We had talked for about a half hour on the phone Sunday, until Mom made me hang up because she was expecting a call. He had said that he really liked me and that we would go out for pizza again soon.

But talking to Randy on the phone isn't nearly as good as seeing him in person. He looked even handsomer than ever with his dark wavy hair and gorgeous blue eyes. I was so much in love I thought I'd die, and I sat there daydreaming about him all through the announcements.

Just then Wiggins called for attention. She had an awfully serious look on her face, and she was standing tall and straight and so still that none of her red corkscrew curls were bobbing around her head. The whole class got still, also, the way we always do when we know there's going to be trouble.

"Boys and girls," Wiggins began in her general's voice. "I have a very serious matter to discuss with you this morning."

I looked at Christie out of the corner of my eye. Since her mother is the principal, sometimes she finds out ahead of time when something important is going on. She looked back at me and then shrugged a teensie shrug that Wiggins probably couldn't see.

"My wallet is missing, and I have reason to believe that someone in this class took it."

My heart stopped, and the back of my mouth got that funny feeling it always gets when I'm going to throw up.

"When I got to school this morning," Wiggins went on, "I put my purse into the bottom desk drawer where I always keep it. I left the room for a few minutes, and when I returned approximately ten minutes before time for the bell and looked into my purse for a handkerchief, my wallet was not there."

Wiggins paused and looked around the room as if she were allowing time for her words to sink in. They sank into me, all right, and that terrible feeling in the back of my mouth was getting stronger. The wallet I found had to belong to Wiggins. And I could feel it sitting there in my jacket pocket like a two-ton rock. What if she searched everyone and found it? She would think I stole it. What would I do then?

She cleared her throat and started talking again. "As I said before, this is a VERY SERIOUS MATTER. I am terribly concerned and would like a private meeting with whoever is responsible. I'm sure we can work out this matter before it gets out of hand and the authorities have to be called. Now, please open your math books to page seventy-five."

I felt like a zombie as I pulled my math book out of my desk and opened it. The authorities? That meant, the police! I went numb all over at the thought of Wiggins calling the police. So numb, in fact, that I couldn't have thrown up if I wanted to.

All around the room kids were looking suspiciously at each other. Lots of kids looked at me. I knew they were thinking that since I was late, I was probably out on the school ground burying my loot or something. I could feel my face turning red and my ears getting hot.

If only they knew.

2❊

*I*t seemed as if morning recess would never come. I looked at the clock above the blackboard at least five hundred times. A few times I was sure it had stopped.

The minute I got outside, I motioned to my four best friends to follow me to one corner of the playground near the fence where we could be alone. We went there lots of times when we had important things to talk about and didn't want anyone else to hear us.

My friends are Beth Barry, Melanie Edwards, Christie Winchell, and Katie Shannon, and we are just about as different as five friends can be. Christie is the math whiz and all-around genius of the group. Also, her mother is principal of our school. Beth is the dramatic one, and I just know that she'll be an actress when she grows up, if she isn't a rock star. Katie is our radical feminist. She has red hair and an Irish temper, and she isn't somebody any of us likes to get into an argument with. Then there's romantic Melanie. She used to be overweight from eating too many of her mother's scrumptious homemade brownies, but now she's losing weight and getting a lot prettier. We call ourselves the Fabulous Five and always help each other whenever we can, which is why I knew I could talk to them about Wiggins's wallet.

Beth fell in step beside me. "Okay, Morgan. What's up ? You've been acting funny all morning."

Beth is on this kick of calling everyone by their last names. She's also on a kick of wearing the loudest clothes she can find. Today she was wearing blinding fuchsia stirrup pants and a matching fuchsia sweatshirt with a gigantic black tic-tac-toe design on the front.

"It isn't funny," I assured her. "It's serious. I know where Wiggins's wallet is."

"What!" she shrieked. "Wiggins's wallet! Where is it?"

"Shut up!" I screeched. "Do you want the whole world to hear you?"

I looked around. No one else had heard,of course, except for Katie, Melanie, and Christie, and now they crowded around me, all talking at once.

"Wiggins's wallet! Don't tell me you have it?" demanded Christie.

"Is the money gone?" asked Katie.

"Are you going to tell us or not?" Melanie pleaded.

"I found it in the girls' bathroom," I said. "I haven't looked inside it yet, but I'm sure it's hers."

I reached into my jacket pocket and slowly extracted the wallet with two fingers. I was almost afraid to touch it after Wiggins said she might call the police. Nobody said anything. They just stared with their mouths open as I opened the wallet. Sure enough, there was Wiggins's picture on the driver's license staring out at us through a plastic window.

"What about the money?" Katie urged. Leave it to her to always think of the practical side of things.

Gingerly I peeked into the compartment where bills are supposed to be kept. It was empty, just as we all knew it would be.

Melanie's eyes were round and frightened. "You were right. This IS serious. What are you going to do?"

"You'd better turn it in," said Christie. "I'm sure if you explain about how you found it, you won't get into trouble."

"Are you kidding?" I cried. "What's to keep Wiggins from thinking that I stole it? And what if after I turn it in, something else gets stolen and I get blamed for that? And Wiggins calls the police? And I get sent to jail?"

"But, Jana," Christie reasoned," You've never stolen anything in your life."

"So?" I said, "Can you think of anyone in our class who has? Wiggins said she thought it was one of us. What makes me so special?"

Nobody said anything to that. I could tell they all agreed. I hid the wallet in my jacket pocket again and thought about Randy. What would he think if I were accused of stealing Wiggins's wallet? He was the nicest boy in the whole wide world, a really kind and sensitive person. He wouldn't want a girlfriend who was a thief.

"I'm not going to take any chances," I announced after a minute. "I'm going to wait until after school when the girls' bathroom is deserted again. Then I'm going to put the wallet back. Only I'll put it somewhere where the custodian will find it when he cleans up later. That way Wiggins will still get it back, but nobody will think I stole it."

"Morgan, that's brilliant!" shouted Beth.

Everybody else agreed that it was a good idea, too, and I went back to class after recess feeling one hundred percent better. The day dragged by, and in the cafeteria at noon all anyone could talk about was Wiggins's wallet.

"Doesn't it feel weird to know that there's a thief in the same room with us?" asked Melanie as we sat at our favorite table eating our lunches. "For all any of us know, we could be sitting right next to him."

"Her, you mean," Katie corrected. "It has to be a girl. Somebody would have noticed a boy stashing a wallet in the girls' bathroom."

We all giggled at that.

"Maybe it's Taffy Sinclair," I offered, nibbling a corner off my cream cheese and jelly sandwich.

"Wouldn't that be great!" said Beth. Her eyes lit up, and she rubbed her hands together like a villain in an old-time movie. "Can't you just see her now, in jail, clinging to the bars of her cell and sobbing her little heart out?"

Everybody was giggling again. Everybody except me. It wasn't that I didn't want the thief to be Taffy Sinclair. It was just that the mention of jail had reminded me of how much trouble I could be in if I didn't get rid of Wiggins's wallet and get rid of it fast. I couldn't eat any more of my sandwich. I couldn't do anything but worry.

Wiggins didn't mention the thief or her wallet again during the afternoon. I guess she thought once was enough. It certainly was enough for me, and when the dismissal bell finally rang and everybody went tearing out of the room, I went, too. I didn't want anyone remembering that I had been late this morning and thinking that I was hanging around to make a big confession.

The halls cleared in about two minutes flat, but I decided to stall at least another five minutes in case someone stopped off at the rest room before leaving for home. I can't remember when I had been so nervous. I stood beside my open locker, rearranging things and wishing that I were a thousand miles away. I had never felt so alone in my life, either. I had told the gang to go on home. They had offered to stay with me, but I said no. I didn't want to draw any more attention to myself than necessary.

Finally I couldn't stand it any longer. The school was as quiet as a tomb. A few teachers were still in their rooms grading papers and things, but all the kids were gone. I tiptoed down the hall and stopped in front of the girls' bathroom door, putting my hand inside my jacket pocket to make sure the wallet was still there. Then I took a deep breath, pushed open the door, and went inside.

It was empty, just as I had hoped it would be. That was a relief. Just to make extra sure, I looked under each stall door. No legs. The coast was clear. All I had to do was leave that wallet where the custodian would find it and get out of there.

I looked around for a good place to put it. I thought about sticking it behind the toilet again. That was where I had found it. But what if the custodian didn't see it there? I couldn't take a chance on that. I wanted him to find that wallet and give it back to Wiggins. That way I'd know I was off the hook.

I decided to put it beside the trash can. It was overflowing with soggy paper towels, and he would have to empty it. When he picked it up, he would naturally see the wallet on the floor. I started to grin. This was perfect.

Digging the wallet out of my pocket, I turned it over in my hand and looked at it one more time. Then I rubbed it against my jacket to get rid of my fingerprints. Good-bye, I thought happily, and good riddance!

I didn't hear the bathroom door open until it was too late. I was already bending down, reaching out in front of me with the wallet in my hand. I dropped that wallet as if it were a red hot poker and spun around. I couldn't believe it. Standing in front of me with a nasty grin on her face was Taffy Sinclair.

3❋

*T*affy didn't say a word. She walked right past me to a sink and ran a few drops of water over her hands. Then she pulled a paper towel out of the holder, dried her hands, and tossed the towel into the trash can as she headed for the door. Finally she stopped and looked back at me.

"Is Wiggins keeping you after school for being tardy this morning?" she asked in her icky sweet voice.

Before I could answer, she was gone. I stared at the door as it swung closed. My mouth was probably open. I couldn't believe what had just happened. Taffy Sinclair had caught me putting Wiggins's wallet beside the

16

trash can. Why hadn't she said anything? Was it possible that she hadn't noticed what I was doing?

Maybe she did see, but she didn't give herself away. Maybe she was telling Wiggins right this minute, or Mrs. Winchell, and maybe they were calling the police. That's probably what she was doing at school so late, anyway. She was hanging around, buttering up the teachers.

My hands were shaking as I pushed open the door and peered into the hall. I wanted to get out of there before Wiggins and Mrs. Winchell and Taffy all came marching into the bathroom and found me and stopped me from leaving before the police arrived. Should I take the wallet with me? No. There wasn't anything I could do with it. If they searched me or gave me a lie detector test, they would know I had it, anyway.

Luckily, the hall was empty. I slid out, looked around one more time, and dashed for the door. All the way home I kept glancing back over my shoulder and listening for sirens.

When I reached my apartment building, I almost collapsed with relief. I had made it. I was safe. Mom wouldn't let anything happen to me. I would explain the whole thing to her, and she would know what to do. I looked at my watch as I unlocked our front door and went inside. It was a whole hour before she would be home from work. In the meantime, I needed to talk to my friends.

Just then the phone rang. I grabbed it and said hello before I had time to consider that it might be the police. It wasn't. It was Beth.

"Morgan! How did it go? Did you plant the wallet? This is the fourth time I've called. I didn't think you'd ever get home."

"I planted the wallet," I said, "but I'm not sure how it went." Then I told her about Taffy Sinclair.

Beth didn't say anything for a minute, which is really unusual for her. Then she let out a low whistle and said, "Gosh, Morgan. That's the pits."

"Thanks for cheering me up. What do you think I should do?"

"Have you talked to Christie yet? If Taffy went to Mrs. Winchell and told on you, Christie could find out."

"Right," I said, even though I wasn't sure I wanted to know a thing like that. "But Mrs. Winchell probably isn't home from school yet."

"Well, I'd better go now," said Beth. "My mom wants me to go to the store with her. Call me later. Okay?"

"Sure," I said. I hung up the phone feeling lonely again. No matter how much my friends cared, there wasn't really anything they could do to help me. Still, I thought, maybe somebody will have a good idea.

I dialed Melanie's number and listened while it rang. Finally someone answered. "Heh-wo." It was Jeffy, Melanie's four-year-old brother. I hated it when he answered.

"Hi, Jeffy. This is Jana. May I speak to Melanie, please?"

Jeffy didn't say anything. I waited for a minute, but he still didn't say anything. I knew why he was still on the phone, but I didn't feel like cooperating.

"Jeffy! I told you that this is Jana. Now will you please call Melanie to the phone? This is important."

Still no answer. I sighed. Jeffy loves to talk on the phone, and he won't ever call Melanie until you talk to him a little bit.

I was getting angrier by the minute. "So what did you do today, Jeffy?" I asked impatiently.

"I pwayed," he said slowly. "And I ate wunch . . . and watched Sesame Stweet . . . and . . ."

"Great, Jeffy. It sounds like you had a terrific day. Now will you please call Melanie to the phone."

Silence again. I tapped my foot. They ought to make it a crime to let little kids answer the phone, I thought. *Crime*. Good grief! I was just about to yell at Jeffy again when there was this ear-splitting crash. Jeffy had dropped the receiver. At least that meant he was finally calling Melanie to the phone.

"Jana? Is that you?" asked Melanie a moment later. "I've been dying for you to call. Tell me what happened."

I wanted to say that if she had been dying for me to call, then why wasn't she standing by the phone instead of letting Jeffy answer it? But I didn't. I told her about Taffy Sinclair.

"You mean she saw you!" cried Melanie. "Oh, my gosh. That's terrible."

Melanie was no help, either. In fact, she made me feel worse than Beth had. All she could do was moan and talk about how terrible the situation was. After the third "that's terrible," I said I had to go and hung up.

But Katie was the worst. "Even if a judge decided you were guilty, you would probably get off with probation," she said matter-of-factly after I told her about Taffy Sinclair and how I thought Wiggins and Mrs. Winchell might have called the police.

"JUDGE! GUILTY! PROBATION!" I shrieked. "Katie, how can you say a thing like that?"

"You have to face the facts, Jana. Wiggins said she might call the police. And you know that by putting that wallet back, you just made yourself look guiltier than ever. So if Taffy Sinclair told what she saw after Wiggins had already asked the guilty party to come forward. Well . . ."

I slammed the phone down without even saying good-bye. I didn't care if Katie got mad. Judge? Guilty? Probation? How could a thing like this be happening to me? I knew I had to call Christie and find out if Taffy really had told on me or not. I tried to reach for the phone, but my hand wouldn't budge. I couldn't lift it for anything, and I knew that even if I did, my fingers would refuse to dial her number.

I'll have a snack first, I told myself. I wasn't sure I could swallow anything, but I went into the kitchen anyway. There was cold pizza in the fridge. The thought of eating it made my stomach turn. I poured myself a glass of milk instead and sat down at the table.

I was sitting there, staring off into space, wondering if Mom would let me transfer to a school on the moon when I heard her key turn in the lock. She was home. I almost couldn't stand it. It was too good to be true.

I raced into the living room to meet her at the door. I didn't want to wait another second to talk to her. But when she walked in, my heart nearly stopped. Her eyes were ablaze with anger.

I gulped hard. "Mom?" I said. "What's the matter?"

I didn't really want her to tell me because I probably knew already. The police. They had been called. And they had talked to Mom.

"Sit down!" she said sharply as she stuffed her coat into the hall closet. "I just got a telephone call that I need to talk to you about."

When I sat down, I couldn't feel the sofa cushions underneath me. I couldn't feel anything except my heart pounding in my chest. Although it was obvious that she was furious, her eyes were red, which meant that she had been crying. I wanted to cry, too. I wanted to tell her not to believe what the police said. Or what Wiggins said, or Mrs. Winchell. I hadn't stolen that wallet. I had never stolen anything in my life. But Mom was talking again.

"It was your father," she said angrily.

My father? I didn't understand. How could he know about Wiggins's wallet?

She sighed and looked at her hands for a moment as if she were trying to compose herself.

"Do you remember the call I got from him a few days ago?" she asked. This time her voice was calmer.

I did, and I felt a sudden rush of relief. The call was not about the stolen wallet. It was from my father, who lives in Poughkeepsie, New York, and never comes to see me and has hardly ever written to me since he and my mother were divorced when I was three. Mom says he really loves me. He's just embarrassed about his drinking problem, but I keep hoping that someday he'll change and we'll really get to know each other.

"Sure," I said. "I remember. He said that he had lost his job again and that he might not be able to pay his rent and that he might need our help." Secretly I remembered that I had almost wished it would happen because Mom had said he might come to Bridgeport. That would mean I would get to see him after all these years. But I didn't say that to Mom. She had been too upset.

Mom nodded sharply, and I could tell that she was getting angry once more. "Well, he called again this afternoon. And he said that he has to move out of his apartment next week if he doesn't get some money to pay the rent. And if that happens, he has no place to go! Of course he'll come here! Oh, Jana. How can he do this to us? He has no right! I just have a little bit of money saved, and we might need it if we had an emergency." She sighed. "But I guess I don't really have a choice, do I?"

I shook my head. "You'd better send it to him. It'll be okay."

She nodded and got up, heading for her room. Deep worry lines creased her face. As I watched her go, a million different thoughts jumbled in my mind. I couldn't tell her about Wiggins's wallet now. She had enough on her mind. I'd have to work that out all by myself.

She hadn't mentioned Pink, but I knew she was thinking about him, too. Pink is the nickname of Wallace Pinkerton. He and Mom have been dating for ages. He took her to dinner at Ricardo's, the swankiest restaurant in Bridgeport, last Saturday night. He even bought her a diamond ring and asked her to marry him a few months ago. Mom said she needed a little more time to make a decision, and I'm glad. I really like Pink. I know Mom does, too. But I have a hard time thinking about him as a father. He seems more like a good friend. Anyway, I know it would be embarrassing for her to have her ex-husband show up when her boyfriend is around.

I leaned back against the sofa and thought about my father. I couldn't believe that he might actually have to come here. It could happen if he couldn't get another job and pay his own rent when it was due again. I felt a little guilty wanting him to come because of Pink and all, but if he did show up right here in Bridgeport, Connecticut, it would be the answer to my prayers. I shot up straight again. No, it wouldn't! It would be awful! What on earth would he think of me if I were accused of being a thief?

I held my breath all evening waiting for the police to knock on the door, but they never did. I didn't tell Mom about my problem, either. How could I when she was so upset about my father? Finally, just before bedtime, I got up enough nerve to call Christie. Fortunately she answered the phone.

"Mom hasn't said a word about Wiggins's wallet," she assured me after I had gone through my story about Taffy Sinclair for the fourth time. "I really don't think Taffy told on you."

We talked a while and Christie finally convinced me that Taffy probably didn't notice that I had the wallet in my hand.

"I'll bet she was too busy looking at herself in the mirror to notice anything," said Christie. "I'll also bet that if you just forget about it, it will all blow over. After all, you put it back where you found it, didn't you?"

I felt a lot better. Maybe it will all blow over, I thought as I climbed into bed. But of course it didn't. Taffy was waiting for me the next day when I got to school.

4※

In the morning I felt a little more confident. After all, Christie was right. I had put the wallet back in the girls' bathroom where the custodian would find it and give it back to Wiggins. Since Taffy Sinclair hadn't told on me, she must not have seen me. I was safe. Then I saw Taffy standing beside the gate to the school ground, and I could tell by the look on her face that I WASN'T safe at all.

"Come here, Jana." She wasn't even bothering to use her icky sweet voice this morning. "I have something IMPORTANT to talk to you about."

"What do you want?" I demanded.

"You'll find out, and so will the whole school if you don't come closer."

I kicked a rock off the sidewalk and moved just close enough so that she wouldn't have to shout.

"I said, what do you want?"

Taffy smiled her nasty smile again. "I didn't tell," she said cheerfully.

"What do you mean, you didn't tell?" I tried to keep the panic I was feeling from creeping into my voice, but I knew it did anyway.

"About what you were doing in the girls' bathroom after school yesterday. Aren't you even going to say thank you?"

"You listen to me, Taffy Sinclair. I didn't steal Wiggins's wallet. I found it. I found it in the girls' bathroom before school. When Wiggins said somebody stole it, I was afraid she'd think it was me. So I put it back where the custodian would find it when he cleaned up. That way I knew she'd get it back. You can think anything you want to, but that's the truth!"

"So you confess!" she challenged gleefully. "You did have Wiggins's wallet all the time. You're the thief, and I'm the ONLY one who knows it."

I stared at her, dumbfounded. She had tricked me. She had made me say that I had Wiggins's wallet, and now she was saying that I confessed. I thought I'd die. I almost wished she had told on me yesterday and the police had come to my apartment and taken me away. At least then I'd get a trial.

Taffy started to walk away. Then she stopped for an instant and narrowed her eyes, looking at me with another one of her nasty looks. "I'll talk to you some more later," she said with a warning sound in her voice. "And like they say in the movies—don't leave town." She was laughing her head off when she turned away again.

My knees felt wobbly as I hurried toward school. I could see my friends standing together near the front door. They had been watching Taffy and me, and I could tell that they were about to explode if they didn't find out what had been going on.

"Do you know what I think?" asked Beth after I had repeated our conversation. "I think she's going to blackmail you."

"Blackmail me?" I almost whispered the dreaded word. Only real criminals did something like that.

" I think she is, too," said Katie. "Otherwise, she would have told on you yesterday. She had this planned from the very moment she saw you with that wallet in your hand."

"But what if Wiggins already has her wallet back?" I protested. "The custodian should have found it and given it back to her already. Maybe she won't care who took it anymore."

"Get serious," said Katie. "The money was gone from the wallet, right? She's going to want to know who the thief is as much as ever."

"Okay, Jana," said Christie. "I think it's time you went to Wiggins and told her the whole story. You know we'll all back you up. We'll tell her that you showed us the wallet and told us what happened and that you were afraid she'd think you were a thief so you put it where it would be found. She would have to believe all of us."

"Yeah," said Melanie. "We should have done that in the first place."

When I didn't say anything for a few minutes, Katie frowned at me and said, "Well? Are you going to do it?"

I shook my head. "It won't work," I said miserably.

"Why not?" demanded Beth.

"Because everybody, including Wiggins, knows what good friends we are and that we always stick up for each other. Besides, if Taffy decides to tell what she saw, then it will be our word against hers. And you know that Taffy has always been a teacher's pet. Wiggins would believe her in a minute before she'd believe us."

"Couldn't you talk to your mom, Christie?" asked Melanie.

"No. She makes a point of staying out of any trouble I'm involved in. She says it's not good policy and that the teachers would resent it if she stuck her nose into their business."

At that moment every bit of confidence I ever had drained away, and a helpless feeling settled in its place. "So where does that leave me?" I pleaded.

Everybody looked at me sympathetically, but no one had an answer.

"I guess I don't have any choice," I said with a sigh. "I'll just have to wait and see what happens next."

What happened next was that Alexis Duvall came running up to us as we headed for our lockers.

"Have you heard what Taffy Sinclair is saying?"

I stopped dead still in my tracks. I tried to swallow, but I couldn't. I could tell that my friends were worried, too. Finally Melanie spoke up.

"No, what? Not that any of us would believe anything she said anyway."

"She says that she knows who the thief is and that maybe, just MAYBE, she'll tell. Can you believe that? There really is a thief in our room, and Taffy knows who it is!"

You would have thought from the way Alexis was prancing around that someone had just told her there really was a Santa Claus. I tried to act excited. I also tried to think of something to say to Alexis that would make me look innocent. I couldn't think of a word. As usual, Beth could.

"Come on, Duvall. You know Taffy. She's always trying to get attention. I'll bet she doesn't know any more about who stole Wiggins's wallet than you do." Then she put an arm around Alexis's shoulder and said in her best Dracula voice, "But if the thief turns out to be you—THEN I VILL BITE YOUR NECK!"

Alexis broke up. She was laughing so hard she had to practically juggle her math book and her lunch to keep from dropping them. I felt a little better, but I still had to face Taffy again. She always got to the classroom early so that she could make points with Wiggins. Her desk was right up at the front by Wiggins's desk, and I had to walk past her to get to my seat. I crossed my fingers three times for luck and made a wish that she wouldn't point to me and tell Wiggins that I was the thief.

Unfortunately I didn't really believe in stuff like crossing my fingers and making wishes, so I wasn't surprised when my friends and I entered the sixth-grade room and Taffy was already in her seat, watching kids come in. Wiggins was sitting at her desk marking something in her grade book; I couldn't tell if Taffy had said anything to her or not.

"Good morning, Jana," Taffy said in an extra icky sweet voice. "Have you been in the girls' bathroom this morning . . . TO COMB YOUR HAIR?"

My face turned burning hot, and I could feel my eyes bugging out, but Wiggins didn't look up from her grade book. That rat Taffy Sinclair was trying to trick me into giving myself away.

"No!" I said. Then I narrowed my eyes and gave her the worst poison-dart look that I could. "I don't spend nearly as much time in the girls' bathroom COMBING MY HAIR as you do."

I spun around, turning my back on her, and headed for my desk. My friends were all grinning and giving me the thumbs-up sign for victory, but I had a terrible feeling in the pit of my stomach. Taffy Sinclair really had it out for me. She had just made that perfectly clear.

Even the 1,000-watt smile that Randy gave me didn't make things better.

When the bell rang, Wiggins did all the normal things. She took roll and made announcements as if nothing in the world were wrong. Maybe she wasn't going to say anything else about her wallet, after all. Of course, I was wrong.

"Class, before we begin our math lesson for this morning, I want to talk to you again about the stolen wallet."

She paused, and I felt a shiver travel all the way up my backbone.

"I have it back, minus the money, of course. The custodian found it after school yesterday in the girls' bathroom. But that does not end the problem. As I said yesterday, it is important for the person responsible to speak with me privately as soon as possible. You may see me after school, or you may call me at home. But please do come forward so that I can avoid calling the authorities."

Even though I was innocent, I had never felt so guilty in my life. Wiggins was still talking about calling the police. What would it be like to be locked up in a tiny cell? Would Mom get to come and see me whenever she wanted to? My hands were shaking as I opened my math book. Probably everyone sitting around me had noticed. How could I possibly get through the whole day?

Just then I saw something on the corner of my desk. It was a note folded about a million times until it was the size of a penny. I had been so busy worrying about going to jail that I hadn't seen anyone put it on my desk.

I glanced at Wiggins. She goes berserk when kids pass notes. Fortunately, she was looking the other way. I opened it quickly before she looked in my direction and spread it out on my lap. It was from Taffy Sinclair. It looked as if my worst nightmare might really come true.

Jana,
  Meet me by the swings at morning recess. This is important. BE THERE!

                                    Taffy Sinclair

5✳

*T*affy was standing beside the swings when I got outside. She is always the first one out at recess because she sits so close to the door. The distance to the swings from the school door seemed like miles, and I felt like a condemned person walking to my execution as I headed toward her.

"What do you want?" I growled as soon as I was close enough for her to hear me.

Taffy smiled. "Just some favors in exchange for keeping quiet about what I know."

"You don't know anything!" I was having a hard time keeping my voice down so that no one else would hear. I was so mad at her that I wanted to die. "I told you what really happened."

"If you're so innocent, then why don't you tell Wiggins?" Taffy paused and gazed off into the distance as if she were seeing a picture in her mind. "She said that if the guilty person didn't come forward, she would have to call the police. Just think what it would be like if the police came to our classroom and began questioning everybody and searching our desks. When they questioned me, I would have to decide whether to tell them or not."

Taffy was obviously enjoying watching me squirm, and I was determined not to let her get the best of me. "I SAID—what do you want?"

"Wiggins gave us a whole page of math problems for homework. I really don't like to do homework, so, since you have to do yours anyway, you can do mine for me. It would be really friendly of you, and I would NEVER tell on a friend."

"I can WHAT?" This time I didn't even try to keep my voice down.

"You heard me," she said, giving me a sinister look.

"And if I don't?"

"Guess. Of course, if you didn't we wouldn't be friends."

I didn't have to guess, but as angry as I was, I couldn't help feeling a little bit relieved. Math was one of my best subjects. If all I had to do to keep Taffy from going to

Wiggins or the police was give her a copy of the math homework, things might not be so bad after all.

"Okay," I said. "I'll meet you a block from school in the morning and give you a copy then."

Taffy frowned at me and shook her head. "No," she said. "I need them today. I'll have to take them home tonight and copy them in my own handwriting. You'll just have to stay in after lunch and work the problems."

"What do you mean, handwriting? We're doing long division with decimals. That's all numbers."

Taffy smiled. "So? I'll bet I make a two different than you do. And a five."

I had to admit that she was probably right. Taffy Sinclair has fancy handwriting with lots of squiggly little curliques and things. Probably her two's and five's were a lot different than mine.

I hesitated, hating to give in to her, but I knew deep inside that I had to. "Okay," I said. "I'll give it to you after school today." Then I stomped off, leaving Taffy standing there all by herself.

When my friends heard what Taffy had told me to do, they were almost as angry as I was.

"See, I told you," said Beth. "She is a blackmailer."

"That fink," said Melanie. "She's going to make you miss the best part of lunch period."

"She's got her nerve," Christie said.

"You aren't really going to let her blackmail you, are you?" asked Katie.

"What else can I do? Besides, if I stall Taffy by doing her homework for her this time, maybe the real thief will confess and then she won't be able to blackmail me anymore."

None of my friends believed that the real thief would come forward and confess any more than I did, and I still had to do Taffy Sinclair's homework, but I didn't intend to give up my lunch period if I could help it. A plan was forming in my mind. When Wiggins announced free reading time as soon as we got in from recess, I put my plan into action.

During free reading time we can either choose a book from the shelves at the back of the room or read one we have already started. Kids were moving around, picking books off the shelf or digging around in their desks for books they wanted to finish. When I was sure Wiggins wasn't looking, I spread my math book flat on my desk so that she couldn't see what kind of book it was. Then I found the homework page and covered the problems with my arm. With any luck at all I could get at least half of them done during free reading period. Then I wouldn't have to give up all my recess time doing favors for Taffy Sinclair.

I was on problem three when disaster struck, and I was concentrating so hard that I didn't know Wiggins had stopped beside my desk. My head was bent over my paper when she spoke to me so that her voice sounded as if it were thundering down from heaven.

"Jana Morgan! Are you doing math problems during free reading time?"

I couldn't very well deny it, but when I tried to answer her, I couldn't speak, either. I nodded instead.

"And what is it that you are supposed to be doing during free reading time? Speak up."

"Reading, Miss Wiggins," I mumbled. Everyone in the whole sixth grade was looking at me, including Randy Kirwan. I was so embarrassed I thought I'd die.

"That's right, Jana. Now put your math book away and begin reading like the rest of the class."

I did what she told me to do, putting away my math book and getting out a library book to read. I scooted down in my seat and opened the book, hoping that Wiggins would go back to the front of the room and everybody else would go back to their reading.

Just then I could feel somebody's eyes burning into me. I looked up. It was Taffy Sinclair. She had turned around in her seat again and was looking straight at me with a nasty smile on her face. I wanted to scream at her to do her own homework even if it meant telling Wiggins that I had found her wallet. But then I thought about going to jail and about Mom crying when she came to visit me and about my father thinking his only child was a thief, and I sank lower into my seat and tried to read my book.

At lunch, Christie came up with a great idea. "We're all your best friends," she said, "and I think that as soon

as we're through eating we should divide up the problems equally. That way we can get them finished and
still have part of the lunch period to go outside."

"I do, too."

"Me, too."

"So do I."

"And then we can make copies for each of us and we'll
all have our homework done, too," I said triumphantly.

"What are best friends for?" said Christie.

"Yeah. The Fabulous Five can handle Taffy Sinclair,"
chimed in Beth.

My best friends truly were best friends.

As soon as we were through with our lunches, I went
to my locker and got my math book. Then I met my
friends at our private spot out by the fence, and we
started on the homework.

There were twenty problems, which meant that each
of us had four to do. That wasn't so bad, especially since
I had already worked two of mine during free reading.
But it was a cold day and windy, and even though I had
on my gloves, my fingers got stiff before I was halfway
through the problems. Christie finished hers first,
naturally, but I was second. Long division with
decimals is easy for me. I copied Christie's answers on a
separate paper for Taffy Sinclair along with my own
answers. Katie finished next. She blew on her hands to
warm them up and started helping Melanie, who is
terrible at math. Pretty soon she was finished and so was
Beth. We did that whole page of problems, copied them

off for Taffy Sinclair and each other, and still had ten minutes on the playground before the bell rang.

I met Taffy at her locker after school and gave her the homework. "Here," I said. "I hope you're satisfied."

"Of course," she said. "And I'll be satisfied again tomorrow after school and the next day, FRIEND . . ."

"What do you mean, tomorrow?" I demanded. "All you said was that I had to do your homework today."

"Get serious," she said. "My silence is worth more than one measly page of homework! I'll let you know when you've done enough." Then she took the problems, gave a little laugh, and walked off, leaving me standing there shaking with rage.

6 ✱

When I got home from school that afternoon, I was surprised to find Mom already there. She was pacing the floor with her arms crossed tightly in front of her, and there was that furious look on her face again.

"What's the matter, Mom?" I asked a little fearfully. "What are you doing home so early?"

Mom stopped and looked at me as if she were so preoccupied with her problems that she hadn't heard me come in. "It's your father again. I called him to tell him that I was sending money. When I told him the amount, he said it wasn't enough, and he may have to come here anyway. Can you believe that? I don't have any more money in my savings account to give him. And besides, what will I tell Pink if your father ends up on our doorstep?"

I could see Mom's point about Pink, but deep down I couldn't help wishing that my father would come anyway. I've never really gotten to know him, and it's hard to explain, but I have this feeling that part of me is missing. For instance, I know lots of ways that Mom and I are alike. We both have dark brown hair, and we laugh the same way. We both hate brussel sprouts and cry at sad movies. But what do my father and I have in common? Is he grouchy when he first wakes up in the morning like I am? Do his ears burn when he gets embarrassed? I don't even know what he looks like now. The last picture of him that I have was taken on my third birthday—just before he and Mom split up.

If only he would come. Even if it were just for a few days. It didn't seem like too much to ask.

Mom was still talking about Pink when I tuned in again. I had missed part of what she said while I was daydreaming about my father. She had said how understanding Pink was but that she didn't want to burden him with her problems, or something like that.

"Maybe you could borrow some money from Pink," I offered. "You wouldn't have to tell him what it was for."

Mom shot me an angry look. "Oh, no. I could never do a thing like that. Actually, I already called the bank and made a small loan. That's why I'm home early. I stopped by to sign the paper and pick up a check. But believe me! This is the last cent Bill Morgan is going to get from ME. He's not going to blackmail me into supporting him by threatening to show up here and ruin our lives."

I jumped when she said "blackmail." Was that what my father was doing? Blackmailing Mom the way Taffy Sinclair was blackmailing me? Pretending to be friends to get what he wanted? I had a hard time believing that he would do a thing like that. Mom had gone off to the kitchen to start dinner, still grumbling to herself about the money, so I didn't follow her and ask her any questions. I was dying to, though.

I couldn't help wondering what *would* happen if my father showed up here. Would he move in and sleep on the sofa? Would he walk me to school in the morning and have dinner with us at night? I got shivery all over at the thought of that.

I went to my room and hung up my jacket. But Mom had used the word "blackmail." I couldn't believe that my father was really as wicked as Taffy Sinclair. What if he really did still care for her, and he was just looking for a way to get to see her? He knows she's a kind-hearted person who could never turn away anyone who needed help—including him. That's it, I thought. Maybe he's just faking needing money so she'll invite him here and they can get back together. It might work out better than Mom thinks, too. I know she wouldn't believe it, but she and my father might even like each other now.

But every time I started to daydream about being a real family again, I remembered the trouble I was in. Taffy Sinclair was the only thing standing between me and jail.

❉   ❉   ❉

Taffy watched every move I made at school the next day, and I watched her back. Every time our eyes met, we sent each other poison-dart looks. There was one person I couldn't look at, though. In fact, I think I would have died if our eyes had met. That person was Randy Kirwan. I couldn't believe that only two days ago I had thought that my life was just about perfect because Randy had kissed me. So much had happened in those two short days! Now I knew I had to keep Randy from finding out about Wiggins's wallet and thinking I took it if it was the last thing I ever did. I was so worried about giving myself away that I couldn't even look at him. The crazy thing was that the more I avoided looking at him, the more he looked at me.

He turned around three times during math period. I know he was doing it so that he could give me his 1,000-watt smile. I could feel my heart doing flip-flops even though I didn't look at him or see that smile. I wanted to let him know that I wasn't mad and still liked him, but I couldn't think of any way to do it without looking him straight in the eye.

At recess I talked my friends into hanging around with Alexis Duvall and her friends, Lisa Snow, Kim Baxter, and Sara Sawyer, so that I could avoid Randy again. Of course, I didn't tell them that I was avoiding Randy. I just said it would be fun to talk to the other girls. It wasn't. All they wanted to do was try to guess who the sixth-grade thief was and look around the playground for new suspects.

"I'll bet it was Mona Vaughn," said Sara. "She doesn't wear very nice clothes, and look at those ratty sneakers."

"You're right," said Lisa. "She probably needs the money. If she comes to school wearing new sneakers, we'll know it was her."

Alexis was looking in a different direction. "Has anybody thought about Stacy Thomas?"

"Stacy?" asked Kim. "She doesn't need money. Her father owns a grocery store."

"Yeah, but she is really mad at Wiggins for flunking her on that social studies test last week. She might have taken her wallet just to get even."

They went on like that during the entire recess, finding reasons why practically every girl they saw on the playground could be the thief. I was glad I was standing with them. I didn't need anyone else getting any ideas about me.

After we got back to our room from recess and began free reading period, Randy started looking at me again. I wanted to look back at him so badly that I didn't know what to do. I tried looking at my desk, at the blackboard, at Clarence Marshall's ears, which stick out really far from the sides of his head, and even at Wiggins, but out of the corner of my eye I could see Randy. After a few minutes he got out of his seat to go to the pencil sharpener. When he came to my desk, he brushed against it. I thought I'd die. He had never brushed against my desk before. I knew he really wanted me to look at him. He probably wanted to talk to me about going out for pizza again, but I just couldn't.

As I sat there, I got madder and madder. Why did someone have to steal Wiggins's wallet in the first place? If they hadn't, and I hadn't found it and got caught by Taffy Sinclair while trying to put it back, then I could look at Randy without feeling guilty, and he could smile his 1,000-watt smile at me, and I could smile back. It wasn't fair.

After he returned to his desk from the pencil sharpener, he didn't look at me one more time all morning. I was nervous when he was looking at me so much, but when he stopped, I got awfully depressed.

"What's the matter, Jana?" Beth asked at lunch. She even called me by my first name, which usually meant she was worried.

"Nothing," I said. I honestly didn't want to talk about it. Not even to my best friend.

I nibbled on my lunch and listened to the conversations going on around me, trying to look around for Randy without anyone noticing. He was nowhere in the cafeteria that I could see without twisting all the way around to look in back. Then I spotted him sitting with Mark and Scott, his two best friends. They were three tables over from ours. He was talking to them and laughing as if he didn't have a care in the world. It was plain to see that he had already forgotten all about me.

I trudged out to the corner of the playground with my friends a little while later and started working on the math homework for Taffy Sinclair. I hated that Taffy Sinclair. Everything that was happening was all her fault. I could hardly concentrate on the problems for thinking about her.

Just then, I felt a poke in my ribs. I looked up and Melanie was pointing toward the bicycle rack.

"Look! There's Randy, and he's talking to Taffy Sinclair."

I heard my pencil clunk as it fell onto my open math book. Slowly, I turned and looked toward the bicycle rack. It was Randy and Taffy, all right. They were standing there talking to each other and acting as if they were really interested in what the conversation was about.

"What do you think they're talking about?" I whispered.

Katie tried to reassure me. "Probably not you. Maybe they're discussing the weather or what they had for lunch."

"Fat chance," I muttered. She's probably telling Randy that I'm the sixth-grade thief, and that she's some kind of heroine for catching me, but that she's too kind-hearted to turn me in."

Nobody said anything to that. I knew they all were thinking the same thing. Everybody knows that Taffy has a crush on Randy and that she'd love to take him away from me.

"Maybe they'll catch the real thief soon," offered Christie.

I was glad that she was trying to make me feel better, but it was no use. There was a lump growing in my throat that was the size of a tennis ball already.

"Maybe," I mumbled and went back to working my problems. I hardly knew what I was doing, and I finished them in about half my regular time.

When everybody else was finished, I started copying the answers off for Taffy. I couldn't stop thinking about Randy and Taffy being together. My eyes were swimming with tears, but I kept on writing anyway, even though everything got so blurry that I had to guess what numbers to put down. I wanted to get it over with as soon as I could, and I honestly didn't realize that I copied every single answer wrong.

7*

When I went to Taffy Sinclair's locker after school to give her the homework, Alexis Duvall was there. Fortunately, Taffy's locker is near a drinking fountain so I stopped at it and hung around waiting for Alexis to leave. I certainly didn't want her to know that I was doing Taffy's homework. I was still feeling rotten about seeing Taffy and Randy together during lunch period so I didn't pay any attention to what they were saying at first. Then Alexis said something that I couldn't help but hear, and I stood up fast and nearly spit out a whole mouthful of water.

"Come on, Taffy. Tuesday you said you knew who the thief is. Why won't you tell?"

Taffy didn't answer for a moment. I didn't know if she saw me standing by the drinking fountain or if she was just being a smarty, the way she usually was. I didn't want to hear what she was going to say next, but I couldn't stand to miss it, either.

"What do you think I am? A tattletale?" Taffy asked in a pouty voice.

"Gosh, no," said Alexis, "but if there's a real thief in the sixth grade and you know who it is, you ought to tell. Whoever it is might steal something else."

"So?"

I glanced at them out of the corner of my eye, and Taffy was giving Alexis an icy look. Alexis shrugged and walked away. I stood there for a minute trying to figure out what I had just heard. Taffy had almost acted as if she were trying to protect me. I shook my head. That couldn't be it. Taffy Sinclair would never protect me in a million years.

"Oh, Jana. There you are."

It was Taffy. She had spotted me.

"Do you have my homework?"

"Here," I said, handing it to her.

She took it, and, of course, she didn't say thank you. I wanted to ask her why she had been so nasty to Alexis, but I couldn't. Part of me didn't really want to know.

❀　❀　❀

"Don't forget," she cautioned as she slipped the homework paper into her notebook. "I'll be waiting right here for you tomorrow after school."

Fat chance I could forget. I thought about Taffy and her lousy homework all the time. I thought about it all evening when I was supposed to be doing my other homework and after I went to bed. I was also thinking about Randy Kirwan. I knew I had lost him, and it wasn't fair. I knew he would never call and ask me for pizza again. Our romance was over. And yet, I hadn't done anything wrong. I had found a crummy wallet. That was all. It was Taffy Sinclair who was doing something wrong. And look at what she's getting out of it, I thought. Free math homework and my boyfriend!

School the next morning started out just like any other day. Wiggins took roll, made announcements, collected lunch money, and then started the math lesson. Everyone passed their homework papers to the front of the room at the beginning of the period the way we always do. Then Wiggins explained the day's lesson and we worked practice problems while she corrected the homework. Just before the period ended, she handed back the papers.

I barely glanced at mine. I knew I had gotten them all right. My friends and I had double-checked each answer yesterday. I heard a shuffling noise up near the front of the room and looked in that direction. It was Taffy Sinclair. She had turned around in her seat and was looking straight at me. She looked so mad that I wouldn't have been surprised if she had started breathing fire and smoke. I swallowed hard. I couldn't imagine what was wrong with her, but there was no doubt about it. She was furious, and the person she was furious at was me.

My friends all noticed Taffy, too. During the next period they kept shooting puzzled glances at me as if to ask if I knew what was wrong with her. I shrugged. Of course I didn't. What I did know was that Taffy had gotten mad right after Wiggins handed the math homework back, and I had a terrible feeling that it was more than just a coincidence.

I was right. Taffy was waiting outside the door for me at recess. She started shouting, and I could tell that she didn't care if anybody heard.

"Jana Morgan! I want to talk to you!"

I hurried over to her before she had time to shout anything else. "What's the matter?" I asked.

"This is what's the matter," she said in a growly voice and stuffed a crumpled paper into my hand.

"Let's go over here where we can have some privacy," I suggested and began moving toward the playground fence. My heart was racing. I couldn't imagine what she was going to say next.

Taffy stomped along behind me, and as soon as we got to the fence I spread out the paper and looked at it. I blinked and looked at it again. I couldn't believe it. Every single problem had been checked wrong! And Wiggins had written a big fat zero in red ink at the top of the page.

"This is impossible!" I shrieked. "All the answers were double-checked. They were right."

"Oh, yeah?" Taffy challenged. "Then why did Wiggins mark them all wrong?"

"I'll prove it to you when we get back into the room. I'll show you my paper. I got one hundred. They were the same answers that I gave you. I swear they were."

"They couldn't be," said Taffy.

"But they are!" I insisted.

Very slowly Taffy pulled another paper out of her jacket pocket. It was the homework sheet I had given her the day before. "Look for yourself," she said angrily.

I took the paper and opened it. I was afraid to look, but I knew that I had to. Glancing down the page, I felt my throat tighten. Taffy was right. It had the same answers on it as the paper Wiggins had marked a zero.

"Taffy, honest," I protested. "I don't know what happened. It was a mistake. It had to be."

"I don't believe you, Jana Morgan. You did it on purpose. I know you did. Don't you know that I could have told on you? I could have gone straight to Wiggins or Mrs. Winchell right after I saw you with that wallet. I could have even gone to the POLICE." Taffy paused, giving me the worst poison-dart look I had ever seen. She had moved so close to me that her nose was practically touching mine. Then her expression changed to a nasty smile, and she said, "I still could."

I knew she was right. She could tell on me any time she wanted to. A picture of me sitting in a jail cell flooded my mind again, and my heart was pounding so hard that I almost didn't hear my own words when they came out. "I'm sorry, Taffy. I was telling the truth when I said I don't know what happened. You've got to believe me. I promise that it won't ever happen again."

"You're right. It won't ever happen again, because you won't be doing my math homework anymore."

"I won't?" I whispered.

"No," Taffy said before I had time to wonder why or feel relieved. "Meet me outside the cafeteria door when the lunch bell rings. I have something else for you to do, but don't think you're getting lucky. Because of what you did to my homework, the price of my silence has just gone up."

8

*T*affy left me standing there alone, and an instant later my four best friends rushed up.

"What's going on?" asked Christie. "Taffy really looked mad."

"She is mad," I assured them. Then I went on to tell them about the math homework. "I don't know what happened. I copied the answers for Taffy from the problems we had worked and . . ." My voice trailed off as I suddenly remembered what had been going on the day before. Taffy had been talking to Randy, and he had been listening as if she were saying something terribly important. It had made my eyes fill up with tears, but I

54

had gone right on copying the answers anyway. Was that what happened? Had I missed seeing the mistakes I was making on Taffy's homework because I was looking through tears? I sighed. I didn't want to admit that even to my friends.

"It serves her right," said Christie.

The others agreed.

"Anyway," I went on. "Taffy said the price of her silence has gone up. I'm supposed to meet her outside the cafeteria door at lunchtime."

"Don't worry, Morgan," said Beth. "We'll go with you. She can't do anything really bad with all of us along."

"No," I said quickly. "I don't know what she's got up her sleeve, but I'd better go alone. She might get even madder if you guys were there. Then there's no telling what she might do."

I fidgeted in my seat all through the rest of the morning classes. I couldn't imagine what Taffy was planning for me, but she had said that it was worse than doing her homework. When the lunch bell finally rang, I hurried to the cafeteria without even stopping by my locker to pick up my lunch. I wasn't the least bit hungry. The smell of Alpo—that's what the kids call the school's meatloaf—was so strong I could have closed my eyes and navigated using only my nose.

I had barely gotten there when Taffy came sauntering up. She stopped and looked around at the kids streaming into the lunchroom. Hot lunch kids were jumping into line in front of the steam tables, and cold lunch kids were scrambling around to find their favorite seats. The room was filling up fast.

Just when I thought I'd explode if Taffy didn't tell me what this was all about, she turned and handed me a hot lunch ticket. "Here," she said. "I'll find us a table while you go get my tray."

"What!" I cried. "I'm not going to get your lunch tray. What do you think I am, your servant?"

Taffy smiled her nastiest smile. "Exactly," she said. Then she pranced into the cafeteria and left me standing there with her hot lunch ticket burning a hole in my hand.

I didn't see where she sat down. I didn't see anything except bright reds and greens and yellows exploding like fireworks before my eyes. Her servant! How dare she tell me that I had to be her servant and bring her lunch tray to her? Who did she think she was, anyway? I wanted to tear that lunch ticket into a million pieces. Then I wanted to stir every one of those million pieces into the goopy mashed potatoes and the carrot and raisin salad and all the other gross things the cafeteria served. But a little voice in my head reminded me that if I didn't do what Taffy Sinclair ordered me to do, I would be in a lot of trouble, so I scuffed into the cafeteria and got in line with the hot lunch kids.

"Hey, Jana. What are you doing in the hot lunch line? I thought you always brought your lunch." It was Joel Murphy. He was standing just ahead of me in line.

I shrugged and turned my back on him. I certainly wasn't going to tell him that I was getting a tray for Taffy Sinclair. He'd probably see me when I took it to her, but I wasn't about to admit it out loud.

I looked across the room. My friends were sitting at our usual table. They were looking at me, and I could tell that they were wondering what was going on, too. This is awful, I thought. It was bad enough when I had to do her homework, but at least then nobody knew. Here I am standing here in front of the whole school being her servant. I felt as if I were on stage.

A minute later I saw Taffy. She had gotten a table near the door where everybody would have to pass by and see us as they went out. Mona Vaughn had just sat down beside her, and they were talking. Why doesn't she let Mona be her servant? I thought. Mona would be glad to do it. Mona Vaughn was really the only friend that Taffy had, and poor, ugly Mona in her old, ratty clothes followed Taffy around like Mary's little lamb. She worshipped the very ground Taffy walked on, and she would probably consider it a privilege to carry Taffy's tray.

By the time I picked up Taffy's lunch and was heading toward her table, Mona was gone. I walked as fast as I could without spilling anything. I wanted to get this moment over with as quickly as possible. Most kids were busy eating and talking to other kids around them. I prayed that they weren't paying any attention to me or what I was doing. I knew my friends were looking. I could see the shocked looks on their faces out of the corner of my eye.

That cafeteria seemed miles long. I thought I was going to walk forever holding that hot lunch tray out in front of me. Taffy was watching me come toward her. She had a look of satisfaction on her face.

"Here," I said, setting the tray down so hard that the silverware rattled. "Now I'm going to sit with my friends." I wanted to get away from her as fast as I could. I could see that lots of kids were looking at me, after all. It was the most embarrassing moment of my life.

"No, you aren't," she said sweetly. I couldn't believe the smile on her face. "Sit down with me so that everybody will think we're friends."

I didn't sit down. I glared at her instead. "Why would I want that?"

Taffy took a dainty bite of her goopy mashed potatoes before she answered. "If you act mad at me, somebody might remember that I know who the sixth-grade thief is and put two and two together."

I felt as if I were sinking into quicksand as I dropped slowly onto the bench across the table from Taffy. She had me. There was nothing I could do but go along. I pasted a fake smile on my face and said between gritted teeth. "I'll get you, Taffy Sinclair, if it's the last thing I ever do."

Taffy didn't answer. She just went right on taking teensie little bites of her lunch and looking up at me and smiling as if we were super friends. I couldn't believe it. She had to be the greatest actress in the world.

"Won't it be fun?" she asked brightly.

"Won't what be fun?" I muttered.

"Pretending we're friends. We can walk back and forth to school together. And we can spend recess together. And, of course, we'll have lunch together every day."

I knew what she was getting at. It was her way of telling me that I would be carrying her hot lunch tray every single day. She was also saying that I would have to humiliate myself by making people think I liked her. It was absolutely the worst thing Taffy Sinclair had ever done to me.

"Don't think that you can get away with this," I said, giving her a big toothy grin for the benefit of anyone who might be watching us.

Taffy laughed and patted her lips with her paper napkin. "I'm finished eating now," she said. "Since we're such good friends, I know you're going to want to take my dirty dishes to the tray return, aren't you?" She actually purred.

I couldn't answer. If I had opened my mouth to speak, something awful would probably have come out. Instead, I stood up and squared my shoulders. Then I picked up Taffy Sinclair's tray and carried it to the tray return with all the dignity I could muster while Taffy waited for me by the cafeteria door.

9 ✻

I could see right then that Taffy Sinclair was going to make a big deal out of pretending to be my friend. Even worse, I would have to swallow my pride and pretend to be her friend, too. It was going to be awful.

When we left the cafeteria together, a lot of kids were watching us. I heard Lisa Snow say to Kim Baxter, "Look at Jana and Taffy. When did they get so chummy?" I wanted to die.

Taffy led me through the halls and outside to the playground. Naturally the sun had come out, and it was so warm that practically everyone in school was out there. I took a deep breath and followed her as she pranced along. She was acting as if we were some sort of parade. She couldn't just stop and stand somewhere like a normal person. Not Taffy Sinclair. She kept on walking around with me right beside her so that everyone would be sure to see us.

Finally, Taffy turned to me and said, "Everyone is looking at us. Isn't this fun?" She was smiling so big that I could see her one crooked bicuspid, which she doesn't like anyone to see. It's the only thing about her that isn't perfect.

I knew I had to smile back so I did it as fast as I could. "Sure," I said sarcastically. "This is the most fun I've had since I had my tonsils out."

At first my best friends acted as if I had positively flipped. They followed us around, staying at a safe distance so that Taffy couldn't hear what they were saying. When they knew she wasn't looking, they made weird faces and pointed in her direction. Then pretty soon they started giving me sympathetic looks. I knew they had figured out that Taffy was blackmailing me again.

Knowing that my friends understood made me feel a little bit better until I realized that Randy Kirwan was noticing us, too. My heart started pounding. He pretended not to, but I caught him looking at us more than once. He was by the ball diamond with Mark and Scott. They were horsing around, but I could tell that Randy was more interested in watching Taffy and me than playing with his friends.

I started to worry about what he was thinking. He knew that I didn't like Taffy Sinclair one bit, and he knew that Taffy didn't like me one bit, either. But he couldn't possibly know that she was blackmailing me. Did he think that I had turned into a two-faced person? Randy is so kind and sensitive. He could never like a girl who was two-faced. Not in a million years.

Then I noticed that Taffy Sinclair was watching me. She had a nasty grin on her face. She knew that I was thinking about Randy. It hit me like a bolt of lightning. That was what she wanted all along. She wanted Randy to see us together. She wanted to embarrass me by making him think that we were friends! That was when she waved for him to come over.

I had to get out of there. I turned around and ran for the door. I didn't know if Taffy yelled at me or not. I just ducked into the school building and raced down the hall. After I turned the first corner, I stopped and caught my breath. I knew I had to be careful. It was against the rules to run in the halls. Besides that, Radar Rollins would be patrolling. He's the science teacher, and kids call him Radar because he has an uncanny way of appearing out of nowhere whenever kids speed in the halls.

The school building was quiet, so I tiptoed up the hall to the next corner and ducked around it, too, in case Taffy Sinclair was looking for me. I wanted to get as far away from her as I could. I leaned against the wall and closed my eyes, remembering how Randy had stared at us. He had a funny look on his face as if he didn't understand what was going on. I knew he thought I was two-faced. He probably thought I hated him because I ran when Taffy called for him to come over to us. He had to think that I was the most terrible girl in the world. My life was ruined. Randy and I would never go out on a date again or kiss again—*ever.*

I thought about Taffy Sinclair, too, and my heart dropped into my shoes. I should never have run away from her. It had probably made her twice as mad as before. What would she do to me now? What if she told Randy about Wiggins's wallet? I needed a plan, something to tell Taffy so that she wouldn't be mad that I ran away. I racked my brain for some kind of excuse.

Suddenly I heard footsteps. They were approaching from the same direction I had come. It was probably Taffy, and she was looking for me. I listened again. It didn't sound like Taffy. She always made a fast, clickety sound when she walked. This sound was slower and heavier. Was it Radar Rollins out on patrol? At least I wasn't speeding.

Just then Mona Vaughn came around the corner. She looked surprised when she saw me.

"Hi, Mona," I said. I was trying to be casual and act as if standing around in the empty hall at noontime was a natural thing to do, but my voice came out in a nervous squeak.

Mona hesitated for a moment. Then she frowned at me and hurried on past. Who cares? I thought, but a

moment later I understood. Mona had seen Taffy and
me together. She worshipped Taffy and was probably
jealous of all the attention I was getting from her.

"Well, she can have it," I mumbled half-aloud.

I was still watching Mona when she disappeared into
the girls' bathroom. I slapped my forehead with the heel
of my hand. The girls' bathroom! Why hadn't I thought
of that? I'd wait there until Taffy found me, and then I
would have a perfect excuse for running away from her.

Mona gave me an even bigger frown when I pushed
open the bathroom door and went inside, so I ducked
into a stall and waited until I heard her leave. Then I
went to a sink and turned on the water. I would stand
there, pretending to wash my hands, until Taffy found
me. I threw a quick grin at myself in the mirror. It
wasn't the cleverest plan in the world, but I knew it
would work.

An instant later the door opened. I held my breath. It
was only a couple of fourth-graders. They were giggling
so hard over some private joke that I don't think they
even saw me standing there. Stephanie Holgrem came
in next. She's in my class, but I don't know her very
well.

I kept on washing my hands. I couldn't remember
when they had been so clean. I kept squirting smelly
green soap on them and rinsing it off and squirting on
soap and rinsing it off until my fingers started to
wrinkle and turn white and the front of my jacket was
splattered with water. Finally the door opened again.
This time it was Taffy Sinclair.

"Okay, Jana Morgan!" she began. She had her hands on her hips and was giving me a terrible poison-dart look. "What was the big idea of running away from me?"

"Emergency," I said. Then I squirted another glob of smelly green soap onto my hands and scrubbed like crazy. It was all I could do to keep from giggling. I stared at my hands and tried to concentrate on washing them so that the laugh that was flooding into my throat wouldn't come bursting out.

Taffy didn't say anything for a minute, but she must have believed me. She dropped her hands away from her hips and sighed. Then she said in a pouty voice, "It's too late to go back outside now. The bell will ring any minute. But you'd better not run away from me again at recess."

Before I could answer, the first bell rang, ending lunch period. I grabbed a paper towel and dried my hands. Taffy must have been perfectly content that she had humiliated me in front of the entire school. Why else would she want to parade me around again at recess? I left her standing in the girls' bathroom and hurried to class, sinking into my seat and wishing I had somewhere to hide. I dug around in my desk as if I were searching for something important so that I wouldn't have to look at any of the other kids as they came into the room. Especially not Randy Kirwan.

I stayed scrunched down in my seat all through social studies period. I was glad no one passed me a note asking what Taffy and I had been doing together at noon, but I was afraid that after they saw us together during the afternoon recess, somebody would.

I looked out the window right after social studies and was surprised to see that it had begun to rain. There hadn't been a cloud in the sky at lunchtime, but there it was coming down softly. As I watched, the rain got harder and harder so that it was practically pouring by the time the bell rang for afternoon recess. I could hardly believe my good luck. I breathed such a loud sigh of relief that Taffy Sinclair turned around in her seat and glared at me as if I were personally responsible for the rain.

"There will be indoor recess this afternoon," Wiggins announced. "You may talk quietly to the people sitting around you, or you may go to the back of the room and choose a book."

Practically everybody in the whole class went zooming to the bookshelves at the back of the room. I did, too, since none of my best friends sits close to me, and I needed to talk to them badly. We pretended to look for books, trying to hide behind other kids so that we could talk.

"What was going on at noon?" Katie whispered.

"Yeah," said Beth. "It looked as if Taffy Sinclair had you on a leash. And, boy, did you run when she waved at Randy. He didn't go to her, though. He just watched you."

"She's making me fake being her friend!" I tried to whisper, but my words came out like an explosion.

"Too much talking at the back of the room," Wiggins called." Just get your books and return to your seats."

Beth was looking toward Wiggins, so I ducked behind Clarence Marshall and poked her on the shoulder. "Tomorrow is Saturday," I said, only instead of saying the words out loud I just moved my lips. "Come to my house at one o'clock for a Fabulous Five meeting. It's urgent!"

Beth screwed her face into a confused frown. "What?" she whispered.

I repeated the words very slowly, exaggerating the way I moved my mouth until she finally understood. She nodded and went to her seat. I gave my other friends the same message, letting them read my lips, too, so that we wouldn't get into trouble with Wiggins.

After I got back to my seat, I realized that I had forgotten to bring a book. I started to go to the bookshelves again, but then I changed my mind. Instead, I began looking around the room and thinking about the real thief. As long as the true identity of the real thief stayed a secret, Taffy could go on making my life miserable forever. It was time for me to do something. That was why I had called a meeting of the Fabulous Five for tomorrow afternoon.

I looked up and down each row of seats. It had to be someone in this class, but the only thing I really felt sure of was that the thief was a girl. I closed my eyes and tried to picture a girl sneaking into the room and stealing the wallet, but the picture was so fuzzy that I couldn't see any particular person. I knew that girls could steal things just the same as boys, but who in our class would do a thing like that?

Just then the door burst open and Mr. Scott, the new assistant principal, came into the room looking very stern. Ordinarily I would have looked at Christie since she has had a crush on Mr. Scott since the beginning of the school year, but he had such an angry look on his face that I watched him instead.

Mr. Scott marched straight to Wiggins's desk, and the two of them talked secretly for a couple of minutes. I could see that Wiggins was getting angry, too. Her face was turning as red as her curls. My heart started to pound. What on earth was going on?

Wiggins stayed seated at her desk until Mr. Scott left the room. Then she got slowly to her feet and raised one hand for attention, which she didn't have to do because everybody was already looking at her. The room was deathly quiet as we waited for her to speak.

"There has been another theft," she said sternly. "This time someone apparently sneaked into the office during lunch period and took all the dollar bills out of the box of lunch money on Mrs. Winchell's desk. I'm asking anyone who knows anything about it to see me after school. We have not yet called the authorities about the wallet theft, but I'm afraid if no one comes forward by Monday, we will have no choice but to call them."

As I sat there staring straight ahead, my whole body went numb. Monday they were going to call the police. This was Friday. Monday was only three days away. I didn't steal that lunch money. Why did I feel so guilty? I knew the answer to that, and it made me feel so terrible that I wanted to put my head down on my desk and cry.

I had come into the school building all alone during lunch period. Worst of all, Taffy Sinclair knew it, too.

10 ✳

"So now you're stealing lunch money, huh?" said Taffy Sinclair as we left the building to walk home together after school. The rain had stopped, but the sky still looked as angry as my mood.

I wanted to scream at Taffy and tell her that I had never stolen anything in my life, but since there were still lots of people on the school ground, I had to keep on faking that I was her friend and smiling at kids and saying, "Bye," and "See you Monday," and things like that.

Taffy was smiling at everybody we passed, too, and talking to me out of the side of her mouth at the same

70

time. "It was pretty smart of you to take only the dollar bills. You can hide those easily. Besides, coins might jingle when you walk."

My hands were shaking so badly that I could barely hold my books. How dare she say a thing like that? We left the school ground and turned a corner. I stopped and looked around quickly. No kids from our school were anywhere in sight. This was my chance.

"I didn't steal that money, and you know it!" I said. "I was in the bathroom. Ask Mona Vaughn. She saw me. And Stephanie Holgrem. She was in there, too."

Taffy had stopped, also. She just looked at me for a moment and then she said, "I've already talked to Mona. She said she saw you in the hall."

"So?" I growled. "You have to go through the hall to get to the bathroom."

Taffy smiled her nastiest smile. "Mona said you acted awfully funny. She said you were leaning against the wall, trying to catch your breath, and that you got really nervous when you saw her."

"That doesn't prove a thing," I insisted.

"Maybe the police would think it does," she chirped. "I'll see you Monday." Then she walked away, leaving me standing there alone.

All the way home I was a nervous wreck. When I got to the apartment I pitched my books onto my bed and headed for the kitchen. I wasn't really hungry, but I couldn't sit still to do my homework, either. I was too antsy. And too *worried*. Would Taffy Sinclair really talk to the police on Monday? What would she say? I knew. She would say that she caught me red-handed putting Wiggins's empty wallet beside the trash can in the girls' bathroom. She would also say that I was alone in the school building during lunch period today and that Mona Vaughn had seen me and that I was acting nervous. Then they would talk to Mona, and she would say anything Taffy wanted her to—even though I knew I was telling the truth.

I poured myself a glass of milk and sat down at the table. Next the police would probably question me. What could I say? I *had* put Wiggins's wallet beside the trash can. And I *had* been nervous when Mona saw me in the hall. I was running away from Taffy Sinclair. But they would never believe that. Not unless the real thief had already confessed, which I knew wasn't going to happen. I swallowed hard as I imagined myself being led off to jail.

I was staring out into space, thinking about living in a tiny cell, when the doorbell rang. It startled me so much that I almost jumped out of my skin. Who on earth could that be? I wondered. Nobody ever came to our house this time of day. Was it the police, coming to get me already? I didn't want to go to the door, but I knew I had to. I stood on my tiptoes so that I could see out the peephole. I almost collapsed with relief.

"Okay, Mrs. Lawson," I called. It was only the landlady.

She was leaning against the other side of the hall puffing and panting when I opened the door. "Whew," she said, handing me an envelope. "It's getting harder and harder to climb these stairs with my old legs, but since this is a special delivery letter, I thought I'd better bring it up."

"Special delivery?" I whispered. I couldn't remember ever getting a special delivery letter before, and my pulse quickened as I saw that it was postmarked Poughkeepsie, New York. That was where my father lived.

"Thanks, Mrs. Lawson," I murmured quickly and closed the door practically in her face. I hadn't meant to do anything so impolite, but this was an emergency. It was a letter from my father.

I sat down on the sofa and stared at the envelope. It was from my father, all right. I'd know his handwriting anywhere. I wanted to open it, but it was addressed to Mrs. Patricia Morgan. That's Mom. It was still an hour until time for her to come home from work. I couldn't wait that long to find out what it said. I switched on the lamp sitting on the table beside the sofa and held it up to the light the way they always do in detective shows, but it didn't work. The writing didn't show through.

I picked at the flap on the back with my fingernail, hoping that it would come loose and open easily. It was stuck tight. That left only one thing to do. I would have to call Mom at work.

"What is it, honey?" she asked after her supervisor called her to the phone. "Are you okay? You aren't sick, are you?"

"No, Mom. It's nothing like that," I said. "It's just that we got a special delivery letter. It's from my father. I thought you might want to know."

Mom didn't say anything for a minute. "You'd better read it to me," she said finally.

I opened the envelope and pulled out the letter. It wasn't very long. I took a deep breath and began reading: "Dear Pat, I am sorry to have to tell you this, but I'll be arriving in Bridgeport Monday on the 6 P.M. bus. I don't have any other choice. I'll only be there until I can get a job and get on my feet again. I know you'll understand. Tell Jana," my voice crackled and I had to stop a minute and clear my throat, "tell Jana that I love her and I'm looking forward to seeing her. Love, Bill."

I heard Mom sigh on the other end of the line. Finally she said, "Thanks, honey. We'll talk about it when I get home."

After we hung up, I read the letter again. Actually I must have read it at least five hundred times. Finally I had to stop because the words were getting blurry from all the tears in my eyes. This was the moment I had dreamed of. My father was coming to live with us. We would get to know each other and do things together. And maybe my parents would even get married again.

So why did I feel miserable? Why wasn't I so happy that I was dancing around the room? I knew why. It was all because of Taffy Sinclair.

11*

When Mom got home she fixed two cups of hot chocolate and called me into the kitchen. The angry look that had been on her face ever since my father first called to say he needed help was gone. That would have been a relief except now she looked sad.

"We need to talk about your father," she began softly, motioning for me to sit down beside her at the table. "I know how much it has hurt you all these years never to have the chance to know him. And I know, too, that you've always dreamed that something would happen to change all that."

She reached over and squeezed my hand as my chin started to quiver. I nodded and watched a big, fat tear splash into my hot chocolate and disappear.

"That's why it's hard to tell you that this isn't that wonderful something you've dreamed of. I'm sorry I lost my temper and said angry things about your father both times when he called, but the fact still remains that it is wrong for him to come here."

She paused. I guess she was giving me time to say something if I wanted to, but I couldn't. The ache in my heart felt like the end of the world.

"I talked all this over with Pink," she went on, "and he's looking for a place for your father to stay. It may take a few days, but in the meantime, it's important for you to understand that your father's coming here is only temporary. He'll be leaving again as soon as possible. I know this is hard for you, Jana," she said gently, "but our life with your father is over for good."

Mom got up and started bustling around the kitchen. I knew our talk was over. I was glad. How could she know how I felt? How could she say that our life with my father was over?

I left my hot chocolate on the table and went to my room. I opened my closet and looked inside. There was plenty of room for his things in it, I thought as I pushed a row of blouses aside. I would make him feel welcome. I would make him want to stay no matter what Mom said.

Next I emptied a drawer out of my dresser for more of his things and then started to pace the floor. I could make everything work out okay. I knew I could if only I could do something about Taffy Sinclair.

The next morning I was pacing the floor once again. I could hardly wait until my four best friends got there for our emergency meeting of The Fabulous Five. I had to talk to them. I was desperate. There had to be something I could do to stop Taffy. My whole life depended on it. I barely heard the phone ring just before noon.

"Jana, it's for you," Mom called.

I frowned. What if it was one of my friends saying she couldn't come to our meeting? Or what if it was Taffy Sinclair with new orders for me and another warning that if I didn't do what she said she would turn me in?

Mom was smiling for the first time since the letter arrived from my father when she handed me the receiver. She had her hand over the mouthpiece. "It's a boy," she whispered. "Maybe it's Randy."

My heart started pounding, and I gave her a tiny smile back. Could it really be Randy Kirwan? It had to be. Who else would call me? But was Randy calling to say he still liked me or was he going to tell me off for being two-faced?

"Hello?" I said.

"Hi, Jana. This is Curtis Trowbridge."

I couldn't believe it. Not nerd-of-the-world Curtis Trowbridge. I hadn't even thought of him. He has had a crush on me forever, and he is always following me around and making me miserable. But why was he calling me now? I had so much on my mind. I didn't want to talk to him at a time like this. I crossed my eyes and made a face to signal Mom that it wasn't Randy. She smiled sympathetically and left the room so that I could have some privacy.

"Hi, Curtis," I said. "What do you want?"

"I'm calling about Wiggins's wallet and the stolen lunch money," he said matter-of-factly.

I almost dropped the phone. "What!" I gasped. How could he know? Had he been talking to Taffy Sinclair?

"Take it easy. I don't know who the thief is. That's what I'm trying to find out. Since I'm sixth-grade editor of the *Mark Twain Sentinel*, I feel it's my duty to do some investigative reporting. You know, that's when a reporter investigates a crime and tries to solve it ahead of the police."

"Oh," I whispered, even though I already knew what investigative reporting was. My heart had practically exploded out of my chest when he mentioned the wallet and the lunch money, and I was still recovering.

"I'm questioning everyone in our class to see if I can get some leads."

"Do you have any?" I asked, hopeful that he did have but afraid they might point to me.

"Not yet. But I've just started asking questions. You're the first person I've talked to." His voice got an official sound to it as he went on. "According to my notes, you came in late on the morning of the first crime. Did you see anything suspicious on your way to class or notice anyone lurking in the halls?"

"No," I assured him. "Nobody was lurking when I came through."

"Nobody. . . lurking," he said slowly, and I could imagine him on the other end of the phone writing that on a notepad. "What about yesterday?" he continued. "Did you go anywhere in the school building after you left the cafeteria?"

I wanted to say no, but I had been seen by too many people to deny it. "Yes," I said softly.

"Where did you go?"

"To the girls' bathroom," I snapped.

"Oh," he said quickly, and I could imagine his face turning red. He didn't say anything for a moment, but then he added, "And you didn't see anything suspicious at the time of either crime? Think, Jana. Even the tiniest thing could be important."

I closed my eyes and thought about Monday morning and how I had stayed late in the girls' bathroom to brush my hair before Randy saw me. There was no one in there but me. *Me and Wiggins's wallet.* And I hadn't seen a single thing that was suspicious on the way to class. I thought really hard, wishing I could come up with a clue. Nobody wanted that thief to be caught more than I did.

"I didn't see anything either time," I said. "Sorry, Curtis. I have to go now. Bye."

As soon as I hung up, I hurried back to my room and flopped down on my bed, staring at the ceiling and thinking about Curtis Trowbridge and his investigative reporting. It scared me to think of him poking around and asking a lot of questions when so much of the evidence pointed to me. He already knew that I was late the morning Wiggins's wallet was stolen. He might think it was because I was taking time to hide it. Now he knew that I was in the school during lunch break yesterday. That meant I didn't have an alibi for either time. Curtis was no dummy. He would figure that out in no time.

What would happen when he questioned other people? Even though she had threatened to turn me in, Taffy might not tell him anything since she couldn't blackmail me anymore if I got caught. But what about Mona Vaughn? She was already mad at me because of all the attention I was getting from Taffy. She would probably think that telling what she knew was a good way to get even.

I jumped up and ran to my dresser, staring at myself in the mirror. "I'm innocent!" I cried. But my father was coming Monday. And with Curtis asking questions, and Mr. Scott saying that they planned to call the police on Monday, I didn't have much time to prove it.

12❋

My friends were all talking about Curtis Trowbridge and his investigative reporting when they arrived for our emergency meeting at one o'clock. He had called every single one of them that morning.

"Don't worry, Jana. Taffy will never tell Curtis about seeing you with that wallet," Katie assured me as we went into my room and closed the door. "She would rather blackmail you than see you get in trouble."

"Unless she gets tired of blackmailing her," offered Melanie.

"Thanks a lot!" I shrieked. "Besides, you only know half of it." I dreaded to tell them the rest, but I had to. "I was in the hall at noon yesterday when the lunch money was stolen, and Taffy knows it."

"You're kidding, Morgan," said Beth. "What were you doing in the hall at noon?"

"Yeah," said Christie. "Did you see who stole the lunch money?"

"No," I said glumly. Then I explained about running away from Taffy and hiding in the school until she found me in the bathroom and about Mona Vaughn seeing me in the hall and telling Taffy how nervous I was.

"Morgan, you jerk," said Beth." How could you get yourself into a mess like that?"

"I didn't know that somebody was in the middle of stealing the lunch money when I ran into the school. I was mad and embarrassed about pretending to be Taffy Sinclair's friend."

Nobody said anything for a minute. Everybody was thinking about how much trouble I was in.

Finally Christie asked the question everybody was thinking. "What if Mona tells Curtis what she saw?"

"Hey, wait a minute," said Beth. "So what if Mona saw you in the hall, Jana? You saw her there, too."

"Sure, but she wasn't acting nervous. And besides, you have to go through the hall to get to the girls' bathroom. That was where she was going."

"So?" challenged Katie. "Maybe she doesn't get nervous. Who knows? Anyway, it's your word against hers. Who else did you say came in the bathroom while you were there?"

"Stephanie Holgrem," I said. "And some fourth-graders."

"Any of them could have done it, and so could anyone else. Nobody said the thief went into the girls' bathroom."

Katie was right. It could have been anyone. Even Taffy Sinclair. What a dummy I was. She had come into the school looking for me and had found me in the girls' bathroom. I thought hard for a moment. An idea was forming down in one of the wrinkles of my brain. An idea about Taffy Sinclair.

"Wait a minute," I said. "When Curtis called, he asked me to try to think of anything suspicious that I saw at the time of either crime, and that's exactly what I did. That's why I missed the most suspicious thing of all."

My friends were all staring at me.

"What are you talking about?" cried Beth. "What did you miss?"

"I was thinking about Monday morning in the bathroom," I said excitedly. "I forgot all about what happened in that same bathroom after school when I was trying to put Wiggins's wallet back. Taffy Sinclair came in! What was SHE doing in there after everyone else had gone home? I had thought at the time that she was probably hanging around to butter up the teachers, but maybe that wasn't it at all. Was she checking to see if the wallet SHE had stolen was still behind the toilet? Had SHE put it there for safekeeping until after school?

Was SHE coming back to get it and take it somewhere where it could never be found?"

Grins were slowly spreading across my friends' faces.

"That has to be it!" cried Christie. "Taffy Sinclair is the real thief."

"Then she got attention away from herself by blackmailing you," said Beth.

"That's right," I said. "I was so busy worrying about what she was going to do to me next that I didn't take time to suspect her of the crime."

"What about yesterday at noon?" asked Melanie.

"That's easy," I assured her. "She must have followed me when I ran into the school and then discovered that she had the perfect opportunity to steal something else and make it look as if I did it. That's why I had to stand around in the girls' bathroom washing my hands about a million times while I waited for her to show up. She was busy taking the money and stashing it somewhere."

I jumped on my bed and started bouncing up and down. My friends all jumped on, too, and we were all bouncing and hugging each other. It was too wonderful to be true. Taffy Sinclair was the real sixth-grade thief.

Naturally, Katie Shannon had to put a damper on things. "Wait a minute," she said. Then she stopped bouncing and got off the bed, turning to face us. "What's her motive? She doesn't need money. Her parents aren't rich, but they're pretty well off. And she has the nicest clothes of any girl in school."

We all stopped bouncing.

"She wanted to blackmail me," I insisted.

"That might be true about the lunch money since she knew she could pin it on you," Katie went on. "But not about the wallet. She was just as surprised to see you in the bathroom after school as you were to see her."

I knew I was frowning, but I couldn't help it. "I don't care," I said. "Taffy Sinclair is the thief, and we all know it. The trouble is, we don't have time to prove it. Mr. Scott said they were going to call the police on Monday if nobody came forward. Now Curtis is doing his best to solve the crime ahead of the police. If he talks to Mona, and then puts that together with the fact that I was late Monday morning—I'VE HAD IT!"

There were nods and murmurs of agreement. "We've got to do something," whispered Melanie. Her eyes were open wide, and I could see that she was just as scared as I was.

"I know," shouted Beth. "We'll frame her!"

"Frame her?" we all asked in unison. I felt little tingles race up my spine. I knew it was against the law to do a thing like that, but it was obvious that Taffy Sinclair was guilty and was framing me. If we framed her, then I would be out of trouble, and she would get what she deserved.

13 ✳

Framing Taffy Sinclair wasn't going to be as easy as we had thought. Nobody could think up a plan that would fool anyone.

"If only I still had Wiggins's wallet," I said. "I could plant it in her desk."

"Maybe you could steal something else and plant it," offered Melanie.

"I'm not a thief!"

"I didn't mean that you were," said Melanie. "I meant borrow. If you BORROWED something from somebody else and planted it in her desk—"

"Forget it," I snapped. "I'm not going to take any chances. It would be just my luck that Curtis Trowbridge would see me. I look guilty enough as it is."

"What if I called Wiggins and disguised my voice?" said Beth. "I could say that I was a friend and that I knew that Taffy Sinclair was the thief. She would never know it was me."

"Oh, yeah?" said Christie. "Wiggins is pretty smart. She'd know your voice in a minute."

"No, she wouldn't," Beth insisted.

"Wait a minute, you guys," I said. "I think I have an idea."

Everybody got quiet. Including Beth, who hardly ever shuts up, even in an emergency.

"Remember how Taffy writes? She makes her letters with squiggly little curliques."

Everybody nodded.

"I think I can fake her handwriting. I'll bet that I could write a note, showing that Taffy was the thief, sign her name, and drop it on the floor beside Wiggins's desk. She'd be sure to find it there. Wiggins goes berserk over kids passing notes, so you know she'd pick it up to see who wrote it."

"How could you fake her handwriting?" asked Christie. "Do you really think you could fool Wiggins? Like you said, she's pretty smart."

"Ordinarily I couldn't write like Taffy, but I still have the note she wrote me the day she started blackmailing me. You know. The one telling me to meet her by the swings. I can trace her letters off that and fake the ones that aren't on it. Nobody writes like Taffy. Even if I didn't get all of her letters right, Wiggins would still think it was Taffy's handwriting."

"You're right," said Beth. "It IS a perfect plan."

"Wait," cautioned Katie. "Who would Taffy write a note like that to?"

I thought a minute. "Mona Vaughn. Who else? Mona is the only friend she has."

I took a sheet of paper out of my notebook and got some tracing paper out of my desk that was left over from a school project. Then I dug around in my jacket pocket until I found the note Taffy had written. I studied it for a few minutes, and while my friends watched, I traced her handwriting exactly and wrote a fabulous note.

Dear Mona,
   I've done it again! I stole all the dollar bills out of the lunch money box. It was even easier than taking Miss Wiggins's wallet, and nobody will ever know it was me.
                                        Love,
                                        Taffy Sinclair

It took me quite a while to write that note, but when I finished and my friends and I looked it over, we knew it was a masterpiece.

"Can you imagine what Wiggins will do when she sees this?" asked Beth. "Taffy will really get it."

"She'll have to pay back every cent of the money," said Melanie.

"I'll bet my mother will suspend her from school for at least a week," bragged Christie.

"I can't wait!" I said. "After all the terrible things Taffy has done to me, it will be fun to see her get what she deserves."

Katie had gotten awfully quiet. She shook her head. "I still can't figure out what Taffy's motive was for taking Wiggins's wallet," she said. "Every criminal has a motive."

"Maybe she'll plead temporary insanity," Melanie said with a giggle.

"And another thing," said Katie. "Remember that Wiggins said that the thief came into the room at least ten minutes before the bell rang. You know Taffy Sinclair. She always hangs around on the school ground flirting with the boys until practically the last bell. Then she waits until everybody is in their seats to make a grand entrance."

"Who cares?" I said. "Taffy has to be the thief. Who else could it be?"

Nobody could answer that.

❄   ❄   ❄

After my friends had all gone home and I had put the fake note from Taffy Sinclair into my knapsack to take to school on Monday morning, I breathed a huge sigh of relief. Everything was going to work out okay after all. Taffy Sinclair would never be able to humiliate me and make me fake being her friend or treat me like her slave again. Best of all, I wouldn't have to go to jail. Other parts of my life were going to be better, too. I would be able to look Randy Kirwan in the eye again without worrying that he thought I was a terrible person. And then there was my father. He would be able to love me and be proud of me and not think that his daughter was a thief. Getting back at Taffy Sinclair was definitely going to be worth it.

Mom knocked on my door a few minutes later. "Jana, would you like to go out to the mall with me?" she called.

I started to say no. Ordinarily I never pass up a chance to go to the mall with Mom. We always stop at the ice cream shop that has forty-five different flavors before we come home. But this time I was still a little angry with her for saying that my father's visit was only temporary. Still, I had to admit that I didn't like it when we weren't getting along, and she was probably trying to make up by inviting me to go with her. "Sure," I said, jumping off my bed and grabbing my jacket from the back of my chair.

We didn't talk much as we got the bus to the mall and then went from store to store. Mom said she had to get new shoes for work because her old ones had a hole in them. I knew Mom couldn't afford much right now since she had sent most of our extra money to my father, so I tried not to look at all the super clothes displayed in the store windows. She couldn't buy me anything right now. Then I thought about Taffy Sinclair. She got everything she wanted, and she had the most gorgeous wardrobe in the entire school.

I was looking at a sweater display in a store window while Mom priced shoes in another store and thinking about Taffy Sinclair when I noticed Mona Vaughn. Mona was in the store standing beside one of the sweater counters. As usual, she looked awful. She had on baggy jeans that were about three sizes too big and a faded sweatshirt.

I was standing there thinking that Mona always wore old, faded clothes and that it was no wonder she worshipped Taffy Sinclair when I noticed what she was doing. She was buying a sweater. It had to be an expensive sweater because it was a beautiful shade of blue with tiny pearls sewn in a design on the front. I blinked a couple of times. What was Mona Vaughn doing buying a sweater like that when she never wore anything half that nice?

I blinked again and looked closer. Mona glanced around the store nervously. Then she very slowly counted out the money for the salesclerk in dollar bills!

I ducked away from the window and hurried out into the center of the mall before Mona could spot me. My pulse was hammering in my ears. The stolen lunch money was in dollar bills, and I had seen Mona in the hall around the time it had been taken!

14❋

I couldn't think about anything but Mona Vaughn for the rest of the weekend. I even turned down ice cream at the mall to get back home and try to figure out what to do.

Deep down inside I knew Mona was the thief. I had seen her give the salesclerk all those dollar bills for a sweater that was more expensive than anything she owned. On the other hand, I also knew that if I told on her, then she would be the one to get caught instead of me. Once that happened, I wouldn't have to worry about getting in trouble, and Taffy Sinclair wouldn't be able to blackmail me anymore.

Wasn't that all that mattered? I kept asking myself. Getting Taffy Sinclair off my back and staying out of jail?

My mind kept jumping back to Taffy. Why couldn't she be the thief? She was so horrible and snotty that she deserved to get in trouble, and I had dreamed of getting even with her practically forever. Mona Vaughn would never blackmail anyone. She was nice. She couldn't help it that she wasn't pretty and couldn't afford to wear nice clothes.

It made me furious to think that Taffy Sinclair was the reason Mona stole the money out of Wiggins's wallet and the dollar bills out of the lunch money box. Or as Katie would say, Taffy was her motive. She was trying to look nice so that Taffy would pay attention to her. *Poor Mona!* She was miserable enough. What would she do if I got her in trouble? On the other hand, I was the only one who knew about Mona. I could go ahead and frame Taffy Sinclair and nobody would ever know the difference.

Mom hadn't said any more about my father since her talk the day before. She's pretty good about not driving a subject into the ground. Usually. But the closer it got to Saturday night and her date with Pink, the more nervous I got about what he would say when he came to pick her up. I couldn't help wondering what he was thinking. Was he jealous of my father? Was that why Pink was looking for a different place for him to stay?

When the doorbell rang at a quarter to six, I raced to open the door. There was Pink, tall and blond, with his usual grin spread across his face. If he was worried about my father, it didn't show.

"Hi, Jana," he said, pushing a pizza box toward me. "Here's your bribe for letting me take your gorgeous mother bowling tonight."

Pink is an absolute bowling nut, and they go bowling almost every Saturday night. I took the pizza, sniffed the delicious aroma, and said thanks. It would be deep-dish pepperoni, green pepper and mushroom. That was my favorite, and he brought me one practically every time they went out.

I took my pizza to the kitchen and dug right in while it was still hot. I was so absorbed in eating that I forgot all about what Pink thought about my father until I heard him say three words: "Alcoholism treatment center."

I put down my pizza slice and listened. "I've called every one in the area," he was saying to my mother. "They're all booked up for at least a month, and a couple of them have long waiting lists."

Then Mom said something about talking about it on the way to the bowling alley, called good-bye to me, and they left. I sat there staring at the door and thinking about what Pink had said. He had been trying to get my father into an alcoholism treatment center. That was like a hospital. I had seen them advertised on TV. I wanted to think that Pink was trying to get rid of him, but down deep I knew that he was really trying to help. Still, he had said that they were all full. I couldn't help being glad. There would be plenty of time for my father to go to the hospital if he had to after we were a real family again.

My pizza was getting cold, so I started eating it and thinking about the predicament I was in. Why did everything have to happen at once? My father coming. Taffy blackmailing me. And now, finding out that Mona Vaughn was the real thief. I couldn't tell on Mona. I just couldn't. If only there were more time. Then maybe she would confess, or quit stealing, or at the very worst, someone else would find out and tell on her. Then I wouldn't have to. But there wasn't more time. My life was going to end on Monday when the police came to Mark Twain Elementary and later, at six o'clock in the evening, when my father's bus pulled into Bridgeport.

When Monday morning finally came, I checked for the hundredth time to be sure the fake note was in my knapsack. There was only one thing I could do, and I would do it all by myself so that if it backfired no one would get in trouble except me.

I got to school earlier than usual. There were a few kids from the lower grades milling around the front door, but nobody from my class was anywhere in sight. I had planned it that way. I tugged on the front door. It was open. I pulled it some more, stuck my head through the opening, and looked in. The coast was clear. My scalp was tingling with excitement. All I had to do was go inside, plant that note beside Wiggins's desk, and I was home free.

"Hi, Jana. What are you doing here so early?"

I jumped so hard that I nearly caught my neck in the door. It was Curtis Trowbridge, and he had come up behind me.

"I just felt like coming to school early," I lied. I certainly couldn't tell him the truth, and I couldn't think of anything else to say. "What about you?"

The grin that had been on Curtis's face changed to an expression of concern. "I'm still working on the case," he said. "And there are a couple of kids I couldn't reach on the phone. Joel Murphy's house didn't answer all weekend, and I got a recorded message saying that Mona Vaughn's phone had been disconnected. I thought maybe I could talk to them before the bell. I hope one of them can give me some clues. Nobody else knows anything."

"I hope so, too, Curtis. See you around." I ducked into the building and away from Curtis as fast as I could. I knew why Mona Vaughn's phone had been disconnected. Her family couldn't afford it, which meant she could never afford to buy that sweater, either—unless she stole the money. If I ever had any doubts that she was the thief, they were all gone now. Not only that, but she might tell Curtis about seeing me in the hall. I only had one chance to get out of this mess. I had to sneak into the classroom and plant that note.

I tiptoed up the hall and stopped in front of the door. The room was dark, which meant that Wiggins wasn't there yet. My hands were shaking as I pulled that note out of my knapsack and folded it up. Then I pitched it underhand and smiled as it landed right beside Wiggins's desk. So what if Taffy Sinclair wasn't the real thief? It was still the right thing to do.

I sneaked back outside, confident that nobody had seen me go inside the building. More kids had arrived on the school ground, but it was such a beautiful morning that everyone was staying outside.

"Hey, Jana."

It was Christie. She and Beth and Melanie were just coming onto the playground. I waved and hurried toward them. Just then Katie came up. All my friends were there and I was bursting to let them in on my secret.

"Come over by the fence," I said. "Have I got something to tell you!"

I explained about seeing Mona buying the sweater and realizing that she had a motive, but that she was too nice to rat on. "I decided to frame Taffy anyway," I said confidently. "She deserves it. I just planted the note beside Wiggins's desk."

Everybody just stared at me for a moment, and then they started giggling. "Morgan, I'm proud of you!" shouted Beth, slapping me on the back.

"I think you're doing the right thing," said Melanie. "Taffy Sinclair treats Mona badly, too. Sometimes she's friendly to her and lets her follow her around, and sometimes she just acts snotty and snubs her."

"Yeah," said Christie. "You're really doing Mona a favor."

Katie didn't say anything. I could tell she was thinking it over.

"Would you rather that I got in trouble instead?" I demanded.

"Of course not, " said Katie. "It's just that it would be better if Taffy really were the thief."

Leave it to Katie to put a damper on things. I wasn't feeling nearly so confident about what I had done when the bell rang. I forgot about my doubts when I got to my locker, though. There was Mona Vaughn at her locker across the hall from mine. She was taking off a corduroy jacket that was so old and worn out that the elbows were shiny. Underneath it was the beautiful blue sweater with the pearl design on the front.

She hung up her jacket and then she started rearranging the books and papers and things in her locker. I knew what she was doing. She was killing time. She was waiting for Taffy Sinclair to come by so that she could show off her new sweater. I would be willing to bet on it. Poor Mona.

I started rearranging things in my locker, too. I had to be sure. I didn't have long to wait. A couple of minutes later Taffy Sinclair came prancing up the hall on her way to the classroom.

"Hi, Taffy," Mona called out. Then she turned and sort of puffed out her chest so that Taffy couldn't help but see her new sweater.

Taffy gave her a bored look and didn't even slow down. "Hi, Mona," she said barely above a whisper. Then she went sailing on by.

I thought I could see tears in Mona's eyes. That Taffy Sinclair was the worst fink in the world.

"Hi, Mona," I called as cheerfully as I could. "I thought the math homework was hard this time. Did you have trouble with problem seven?" I don't know why I said that. The math homework was easy, and I didn't even remember what problem seven was. The truth was, I wanted to say something to Mona. Anything to make her forget about Taffy Sinclair.

Mona gave me a surprised look. Then she smiled shyly and said, "I didn't have much trouble with the homework. You can look at my problem seven if you want to."

I said thanks and walked with her to the room. Mona looked around proudly when we walked in together. I knew she wanted everybody to see that she had a friend. My heart was just about breaking for her. The Fabulous Five would have to be nicer to her from now on.

Wiggins was already seated at her desk, shuffling through some papers. I ducked into my own seat. This was it. The big day. I glanced toward the spot where I had put the fake note. It was gone! Wiggins had found it. Taffy Sinclair's doom was sealed at last. She would never blackmail anyone again. My friends had noticed it, too, and Beth turned around and gave me a thumbs-up victory sign.

Now all I had to do was wait for Wiggins to announce that the thief had been caught. Or for Mrs. Winchell to come into the room with the police. I was so excited I couldn't sit still.

Wiggins made all the announcements and collected the lunch money without saying a thing. I couldn't believe it. Could somebody else have found the note? I thought about that for a while. Wiggins was always the first one in the room in the morning. And I had left it right beside her desk where she couldn't miss it.

That was the longest morning of my life. Wiggins conducted class as if nothing had happened. We went through a boring social studies lesson and forty-two spelling words before recess. I kept waiting for her to say something, but she didn't.

Then the recess bell rang. Wiggins held up her hand and got slowly to her feet. "I'd like to see Taffy Sinclair in the room during recess," she said calmly.

This was it! Wiggins *had* found the note, after all. Taffy's eyes were wide and she had a puzzled look on her face. I stuck my nose in the air when I walked past her. I had done it. I had gotten my revenge on Taffy Sinclair. It was the most wonderful moment of my life.

I felt just about nine feet tall as I went out for recess. I couldn't even feel the ground beneath my feet. I would never have to worry about what anyone thought of me again. I could look Randy straight in the eye. I wasn't guilty of anything bad, and what was more, no one could convince him that I was.

I thought about my father, too, and I breathed a huge sigh of relief. Now he could be proud of me, and if he and Mom decided to get married again, I'd be the best daughter anyone could ever be.

When I got to the playground my friends were all clustering around me. "You did it!" shouted Christie. We started jumping up and down and laughing.

Suddenly I stopped. "I wonder what Wiggins is doing to Taffy Sinclair right now?" I couldn't forget about her for even one second.

"Probably giving her a lecture about stealing," said Christie.

"And Taffy is crying and sobbing and carrying on," Melanie said gleefully.

"And Wiggins is holding the fake note under her nose and ordering her to confess that she's the thief!" I cried.

"What fake note?"

My friends and I all froze on the spot. In our excitement we hadn't noticed Mona Vaughn standing close by. She must have thought that I was her new friend and had followed me out of the room. Now she was standing about three feet from us, and she was looking at us as if she couldn't believe what she had just heard.

"I SAID, what fake note?" she demanded. "I heard you. You said something about a fake note and about Wiggins ordering Taffy to confess that she's the thief. What have you done to Taffy? How could you be so cruel?"

"You . . . you must have misunderstood." I fumbled for words. "I didn't say FAKE note. I just said note. I saw it on Wiggins's desk as I came out for recess. I read it. It was from Taffy and it said she was the thief." I knew I was talking too fast, but I couldn't slow down. The words were tumbling out before I could stop them. I couldn't let Mona know what had really happened. She wouldn't understand—even though I had partly done it for her.

"What do you care?" snapped Beth. "She treats you awful most of the time. Do you think we can't see that? Everybody notices. Taffy treats you like dirt."

Tears were streaming down Mona's face. "How can you say that? She isn't perfect, but Taffy is my friend," she insisted. Then she turned and looked at me with poison-dart eyes. "How could you do such a thing, Jana Morgan, when Taffy was trying to be your friend, too?"

Her words hit me like a bucket of cold water. I wanted to scream at her and say that if Taffy wanted to be my friend she certainly had a funny way of showing it. But I didn't. I couldn't help remembering all the times I had thought that Taffy Sinclair didn't know the first thing about making friends. Still, I couldn't stand to think that she really wanted to be friends with me.

Mona wiped the tears off her face with the back of her hand as she turned and started to walk away. After a few steps she stopped and looked at me again. "Just because you hate Taffy Sinclair, that doesn't make what you did right. I'm the one who took the money from Wiggins's wallet and from the lunch money box. I have to tell Wiggins the truth now. I can't let Taffy take the blame for something she didn't do."

15❋

My friends and I watched Mona head toward the school, scuffing up little clouds of dust with every step. As hard as I tried to shut them out, her angry words kept ringing in my ears. JUST BECAUSE YOU HATE TAFFY SINCLAIR, THAT DOESN'T MAKE WHAT YOU DID RIGHT.

Part of me wanted to shout after Mona and tell her that she was wrong. Taffy Sinclair deserved to be framed. She had been blackmailing me, hadn't she? And she was snotty and stuck-up, and she wanted to take Randy Kirwan away from me. Still, another part of me knew that what Mona said really was true. My framing Taffy was no more right than her blackmailing me. In fact, it made me just as mean and spiteful as she was. I remembered all the times I had heard people say that two wrongs don't make a right, but I had never totally understood what that meant until now.

"She's really mad," said Christie.

"I guess framing Taffy Sinclair wasn't such a good idea after all," I admitted.

My friends all nodded. I could see by the guilty expressions on their faces that they had been thinking the same thing I had.

For the millionth time in my life, I tried to figure out Taffy Sinclair. Was Mona right about her, too? Did Taffy really want to be friends? She certainly wanted people to think that we were. I thought about how she made me sit with her in the cafeteria and how she paraded me around on the playground at noon. There were plenty of other things that she could have blackmailed me into doing that wouldn't have made it look as if we were friends. It didn't make sense. Why couldn't she see that she already had a super friend in Mona?

When the bell rang and my friends and I were walking back toward the door, a terrible thought occurred to me that made me forget all about my guilty conscience and trying to figure Taffy out. "What if Mona tells Wiggins that we wrote that fake note?" I cried.

"Mona may not tell Wiggins, but she'll certainly tell Taffy. And you can bet that Taffy will tell," said Katie.

"She'd die before she'd let Wiggins think she did anything wrong."

Melanie gasped. "Oh, my gosh! Then we'll be in more trouble than Taffy."

"Take it easy, Edwards," said Beth. "We'll think of something."

But we didn't because there wasn't time. We had to go back into class. I felt like a zombie as I marched to my seat. Wiggins was sitting at her desk thumbing through the reading book as if nothing had happened. I wasn't fooled. Mona's eyes were red from crying, and I didn't dare look at Taffy Sinclair. I didn't look at Randy, either, even though I knew he was watching me. I had thought my troubles with him would be over once I fixed things so that Taffy couldn't blackmail me anymore. I was wrong. I had not only made things worse by framing Taffy, but now I was going to get caught. The way things were going, I might never be able to look Randy in the eye again.

All morning long, I waited for Wiggins to call my friends and me up to her desk, but she didn't. I knew she wouldn't make any announcements about the thief confessing. She wouldn't want anyone to figure out that it was Mona. Wiggins was nice about things like that. But she would never let anyone get away with something so horrible as framing another person. It was just a matter of time until she got us.

I kept remembering that it was just one week ago today that my troubles had started. That was the day I found Wiggins's wallet in the girls' bathroom. If only I had just turned it in when I found it. Then none of this would have ever happened.

A couple of times I thought I caught Wiggins looking at me. Was she thinking about what a horrible person I was? Maybe she was trying to figure out how to punish my friends and me so that we would never do something so terrible again.

I held my breath when the lunch bell rang. Still Wiggins didn't call us to her desk.

"What's she waiting for?" I cried as my friends and I headed into the cafeteria.

"Maybe she just wants to watch us squirm," offered Christie as she picked up a carton of milk.

"Or maybe she's going to call our parents to come in for a conference after school and talk to us then," said Katie.

"Oh, no!" said Melanie. "I'll die if my parents find out about this."

Suddenly I stopped dead in my tracks. "Look who's waiting for us at our table," I whispered. I couldn't believe my eyes. It was Mona Vaughn and Taffy Sinclair.

Mona's eyes weren't red anymore and she was looking adoringly at Taffy, but Taffy wasn't paying the least bit of attention to her. She was looking at me and smiling her nasty smile.

"What do you want?" I grumbled.

"I thought you'd like to know what went on at recess, since you had such a big part in it," Taffy said.

I felt my face turn red and my ears get hot, and I couldn't answer her.

"Mona confessed to Wiggins that she's the thief. Wiggins talked to Mrs. Winchell and they are going to let her work off the money by correcting papers and erasing the boards and things like that," said Taffy. "Isn't that nice of Wiggins? She could have called the police."

I winced at the word "police." Taffy was getting at something, and I almost didn't want to know what it was.

"Yeah. That's really nice, Mona," I said. "I'm glad she was so understanding."

Mona nodded shyly.

"That's not all," said Taffy. "I thought you would also like to know what happened about the note."

This was it. She was going to zap me now. I knew it had to happen. My friends and I exchanged glances. They were worried, too.

Taffy leaned toward me, looking me straight in the eye. "When Mona confessed, Wiggins realized that when I wrote that note I was trying to take the blame for Mona. She was awfully impressed. Now she thinks I'm the most super FRIEND anyone could ever have."

My mouth dropped open so far that my chin nearly banged on the table. I didn't know whether to laugh or cry. Taffy hadn't told on us. She had pretended that fake note was really from her!

Taffy and Mona didn't stick around our table to see what anyone would say. I watched them go feeling more confused than ever before. I wanted to hate Taffy Sinclair for making Wiggins think she was some kind of heroine, but at the same time, she had saved my life. Was that why she had put extra emphasis on the word "friend"? Well, at least one thing was certain, I thought. Taffy Sinclair would not be able to blackmail me anymore.

16*

*B*ecause of Taffy Sinclair I had hardly had time to think about the fact that my father was coming on the 6 P.M. bus, and all the way home from school I practiced what I would say to him. First, I would give him a hug, and then I would tell him how glad I was to have him back home. Or maybe I should shake his hand instead of giving him a hug. Mom might not be ready for the hug part yet.

I looked at my watch. It was almost four. I didn't have a lot of time. I wanted to fix myself up before we went to meet the bus. I was going to wear my best plaid skirt

111

and matching sweater, and I would borrow Mom's curling iron to fix my hair.

The phone was ringing when I let myself into the apartment. I dashed across the room to answer it.

"Hello," I said between gulps of air.

There was a pause and then a voice I hadn't heard in a long time said, "Jana, honey? Is that you?"

It was my father. I would know his voice anywhere. "Yes, it's me. Is that YOU?"

He laughed softly. "Is your mother home yet?" he asked. "I phoned her office, but they said she had already left."

"No, she isn't here yet. But where are you?" I paused as a terrible thought occurred to me. "Aren't you on the bus?"

I knew what he would say before he said it, and hot tears flashed into my eyes.

"I'm not coming, Jana." I heard him sigh. "I'm sorry. I really did want to see you again."

"Why aren't you coming?" I cried. "I thought you needed us!"

"Listen carefully," he said. "It has nothing to do with how much I love you. I found a job. Isn't that great? Right here in Poughkeepsie. I'm going to get to stay in my apartment after all."

I couldn't answer. I didn't want him to stay in Poughkeepsie. I wanted him to come here. Today. On the six o'clock bus.

Just then Mom got home. I think she knew from the look on my face who was on the phone. I handed her the receiver without a word and went to my room. Slowly I opened the closet door and looked at the space I had made for his clothes. He wouldn't need it now. He wouldn't need the drawer I had emptied, either. He wouldn't need anything from me because he was going to stay in Poughkeepsie instead of coming here so that we could be a real family again. I slammed the closet door and threw myself across my bed.

A little while later Mom knocked on my door. After I said, "Come in," she sat down on the side of the bed and took my hand in hers.

I lifted my face out of my pillow and looked at her. "Why did he have to find a job up there?" I asked.

"I know you're disappointed," she said. "I also know that your dad really wanted to see you, but I hope you'll be able to be happy for him now."

"Why?" I asked.

"Because he's finally learning to take some responsibility for himself. He's figured out that no one else can do it for him. I'm sure he's going to have a much happier life now."

We talked for a while, and I started to feel a lot better. I was beginning to understand what she meant about taking responsibility. My life would have been a lot happier lately if I had taken the responsibility of turning Wiggins's wallet in when I found it instead of trying to push it off on somebody else. I could see that all my misery over Taffy Sinclair blackmailing me was really my own fault. I didn't tell Mom about that. Some things are better off staying secret.

When the phone rang a little while later, I rushed to answer it. I hoped it was one of my friends. I had so much to tell them.

"Hi, Jana. This is Randy. Can you talk?"

My heart started doing flip-flops, the way it always did when he gave me his 1,000-watt smile. But what if he was calling to say he had found out that I wasn't the kind and sensitive person he had thought I was? What if he said that he didn't like me anymore? That he liked Taffy Sinclair instead. After all, I had seen him talking to her a couple of times. I didn't want to know a thing like that, but I had to find out.

"Sure," I said, holding my breath.

"I'm calling to ask you what I've done. Every time I look at you, you look away. Don't you like me anymore?"

"Of course, I still like you," I said, and the breath I had been holding exploded in a happy sigh. "I'm sorry if I've been acting funny lately. You see, I thought my father was going to come and see me, but he's not."

That wasn't quite the truth, but it was close enough. I couldn't let Randy think he had done anything wrong. And I certainly couldn't tell him about Wiggins's wallet or about being blackmailed by Taffy Sinclair.

"I'm sorry your father isn't coming," he said. "And, Jana," he hesitated a second and then added, "I'm glad that everything ELSE is okay." I blushed when he said that, but I could tell he really meant it. Randy is the kindest and most sincere person in the world.

My life was perfect again. Everything was okay between Randy and me. We talked on the phone for ages, and I'll bet it won't be long until he asks me out and maybe even kisses me again! It made me a little sad that my father wouldn't be coming to see me, at least not right away, but I was glad his life was getting happy, too. And as for Taffy Sinclair—my troubles with her were over—at least for now.

ABOUT THE AUTHOR

BETSY HAYNES, the daughter of a former newswoman, began scribbling poetry and short stories as soon as she learned to write. A serious writing career, however, had to wait until after her marriage and the arrival of her two children. But that early practice must have paid off, for within three months Mrs. Haynes had sold her first story. In addition to a number of magazine short stories and the Taffy Sinclair series, Mrs. Haynes is also the author of *Spies on the Devil's Belt* and the highly acclaimed *Cowslip*. She lives in Colleyville, Texas, with her children and husband, a businessman who is the author of a young adult novel.

☐ **TAFFY SINCLAIR AND THE**   **15494/$2.50**
ROMANCE MACHINE DISASTER
by Betsy Haynes

Taffy Sinclair is furious. Her rival, Jana Morgan, has a date with Randy Kirwan, the most popular boy at school. When their teacher conducts a computer match-up game, Jana and 9 other girls, including Taffy turn out to be just right for Randy. Jana vows to win him! But is she any match for Taffy?

☐ **THE AGAINST TAFFY**   **15413/$2.50**
SINCLAIR CLUB
by Betsy Haynes

It was bad enough when Taffy Sinclair was just a pretty face. But now she's gone and developed a figure! This calls for drastic measures from the Against Taffy Sinclair Club made up of Jana Morgan and her four fifth-grade friends.

☐ **TAFFY SINCLAIR**   **15417/$2.50**
STRIKES AGAIN
by Betsy Haynes

It is time gorgeous Taffy Sinclair had a little competition. That's what Jana and her friends decide to give her when they form a club called The Fabulous Five. But when the club's third meeting ends in disaster, Jana finds she has four new enemies!

☐ **TAFFY SINCLAIR,**   **15330/$2.50**
QUEEN OF THE SOAPS
by Betsy Haynes

What could be worse? The snooty but perfectly gorgeous Taffy has done it again—she's won a part in a soap opera to play a beautiful girl on her deathbed. Nothing like this ever happens to Jana Morgan or her friends, and they're not going to stand being upstaged one more time!

BANTAM SKYLARK BRINGS YOU FABULOUS FAMILY FUN FROM CLAUDIA MILLS!

☐ **15397 BOARDWALK WITH HOTEL $2.50**
11-year-old Jessica Jarrell never minded being adopted until she hears something very disturbing from her babysitter. Do the Jarrells really wish they'd never adopted her? Well, if Jessica can't be the most loved one in the family she'll have to settle for something else—the most noticed!

☐ **15499-0 THE SECRET CAROUSEL $2.50**
Lindy is miserable, stuck in tiny Three Churches, Iowa while her lucky sister Joan is off studying ballet in New York. But when she discovers a beautiful old carousel in an abandoned warehouse, she also uncovers a secret about it that will change her whole life!

☐ **15511 ALL THE LIVING $2.50**
10-year-old Karla Myers and her younger brother Jamie are off for a wonderful summer. Their family has inherited a cabin on Lake Mooselookmeguntic in Maine, and now they're going to have a terrific time of swimming, exploring and driving their poor parents crazy in this very funny story of family ties!

Prices and availability subject to change without notice.

Shop at home
for quality children's books
and save money, too.

Now you can order books for the whole family from Bantam's latest catalog of hundreds of titles including many fine children's books. *And* this special offer gives you an opportunity to purchase a Bantam book for only 50¢. Here's how:

By ordering any five books at the regular price per order, you can also choose any other single book listed (up to a $5.95 value) for just 50¢. Some restrictions do apply, so for further details send for Bantam's catalog of titles today.